D1554715

FLIGHT INTO SPRING

Also by Bianca Bradbury

Goodness and Mercy Jenkins
The Undergrounders

Flight
into
Spring

Bianca Bradbury

BETHLEHEM BOOKS · IGNATIUS PRESS
BATHGATE   SAN FRANCISCO

Cover art © 2005 Mary Beth Owens
Cover design by Theodore Schluenderfritz
Inside decorations by Roseanne Sharpe

First Bethlehem Books Printing May 2005

ISBN 1-932350-01-2
Library of Congress Catalog Number: 2005923034

Bethlehem Books • Ignatius Press
10194 Garfield Street South
Bathgate, North Dakota 58216
www.bethlehembooks.com
1-800-757 6831

Printed in the United States on acid-free paper

FLIGHT INTO SPRING

Chapter One

"THIS IS THE longest war that ever was," Sally Day Hammond said gloomily.

Her mother flashed her a warning look. The family had agreed not to discuss the war while Sally Day's cousin Tillman was visiting. "It's the longest winter that ever was, that's true," she said.

Her daughter had caught the warning and said with a smile, "Anyway it doesn't seem so cold tonight, Mama. We've got a lovely supper inside us."

They were all crowded around the kitchen stove, forming three circles. The two hounds were closest because they didn't mind getting scorched. Eleven-year-old Willie, Sally Day's sister, and nine-year-old Eugene huddled close to the dogs. Grownups formed the outer circle. Tillman Wyatt had the best chair because he was a soldier, home for a little while from the war. Mrs. Hammond was sewing in the soft yellow glow of the lamp. Her husband watched them all carefully and Sally Day knew he was afraid the children would ask their cousin about battles and fighting.

As for Sally Day, she was trying not to glance at Tillman, for when she did it was another soldier she saw. That one was just as tall, but dark instead of blond. He wore the blue

Union uniform instead of the nut brown of the Confederacy. Wherever Charles Horne was, this winter night of 1865, he carried Sally Day's heart with him.

War was in the very air the Hammond family breathed, for they lived in Chesapeake City, Maryland. The state was split right down the middle in its loyalties, and had been ever since the War Between the States began in 1861. Sally Day's own father was loyal to the Union and President Abraham Lincoln. Tillman Wyatt's branch of the family was just as loyal to the South. By rights Sally Day ought to hate this tall, handsome cousin. What if he and Charles Horne met in battle? They would be duty bound to try to kill each other.

Yet how could she hate Tillman? They had been friends since they were babies.

He stared into the stove's red glow. He still looked sick and exhausted, despite the good supper Mrs. Hammond had set before him. His blue eyes were haunted; some terrible memories were mirrored in them. How old did he look tonight, with deep lines spoiling his smooth, young face? At least thirty, Sally Day realized. Yet she knew for a fact he was only three years older than she, and Sally Day had turned sixteen not long before.

"Where did you get all that good food, Papa?" she asked, just to make conversation.

Her father seemed relieved that the long silence was broken. "I put over a real good deal today," he said. "A farmer from the back country came to the store to swap a side of bacon for a new spade. He didn't have any cash, of course. Nobody has any cash these days. I couldn't keep the store going if people didn't come in to barter.

"His wife was wearing a plain calico bonnet, and she kept

eyeing that green velvet one that's on the top shelf. I kind of guessed she had never owned a real fancy bonnet in her whole life. 'It's right pretty, isn't it, ma'am?' I said to her.

" 'It surely is,' she agreed. 'Would you take a pound of butter for it?'

" 'I'd take two pounds of butter and three dozen eggs,' I told her.

"Her husband figured that was too much, but I wasn't too anxious to let it go. I'd been thinking somebody in my own family would look right nice in that velvet bonnet. Still and all, I remembered that Tillman was staying for supper, and the rest of us were sick and tired of plain hoe cake. I let her have it for the butter and eggs."

"It was surely a wonderful supper," his wife agreed. "We'll have another tomorrow if Tillman can see his way clear to stay. Tillman, there's an old rooster pecking around the back porch, and I'll have your uncle kill it if you'll stay. What would you say to a boiled chicken dinner?"

It seemed as though Tillman had to come back a long, long distance before he answered. Then with his usual courtesy he said, "I thank you kindly, Aunt Sarah, and it's a fine offer, but I'll be on my way at dawn."

There was bitterness in his voice as he added, "My own town and my own state aren't very cordial to soldiers who don't wear blue and talk with a Yankee twang. I'd best not stay."

"You won't see your own mother, Tillman?"

"No, I don't dare go into Chesapeake City. I'd take it kindly if you'd let her know I'm alive and well."

"That we'll be happy to do," his aunt said gently.

"Aunt Sarah, would you allow Sally Day to walk with me now, just to the canal and along the towpath? The moon's bright as day. I won't keep her out long."

Sally Day was startled by her cousin's request to walk out with him, and her face must have showed it. "It's a cold night," her father said, guessing she didn't want to go.

"It's not too cold if I borrow Mama's cape with the hood," Sally Day said, and stood up. She had seen the pleading in Tillman's eyes.

"Tillman, you had best wear my coat," Mr. Hammond said, and took it down from the hook and put it around the young man's shoulders.

They were walking through the back garden when Tillman stopped short. "What did Uncle George have in mind?" he asked. "Did he want me to cover my uniform? Are you ashamed to be seen with me?"

"No," Sally Day told him, "Papa only wants you to be warm."

"Do the Yankees keep a guard on the canal?"

"We haven't seen any guards for a long time. Weeks, anyway. The war's—"

"The war's what?" Tillman demanded. "Finish what you started to say."

Maybe Sally Day was small, but she was spirited enough to stand up to any man. "The war's nearly over, that's what I was going to say."

"And we're beaten? Do you honestly believe that the South is beaten?"

"Yes, that's just what I do believe."

"It's not true," he said harshly. "That's only Yankee talk."

"Tillman, if you asked me to come outside so you could lecture me on politics, then we'll go back right now!"

He towered over her. The anger went out of him, and he touched her face with his finger. "You're all silvery from the moonlight," he said, "You're so tiny, Sally Day. And I'd forgotten that you look like a little madonna. How could I forget that when I've thought of you every single day I've been away?"

"Now, Tillman," she said with an uncertain laugh, "don't you sweet-talk me."

They started along the wooden duckwalk which Mr. Hammond had built to cross a marshy spot between the back garden and the canal. Their footsteps echoed and Sally Day shivered, hoping they wouldn't see the dark form of a Union sentry pacing along the canal. They reached the bank and to her relief she saw that the towpath was empty.

Tillman took her hand and they walked in silence. Finally he said, "Sally Day, I heard a queer rumor way down in Virginia. That's one reason I asked for a few days' furlough and came home. A friend in my company got a letter from home, and in it there was a mention you were promised to a soldier."

Sally Day's heart began to beat faster. Was she promised? Yes, she supposed she was.

Her cousin went on, "To a Yankee soldier."

"I met one I like, that is true," she said steadily, lifting her chin.

"You couldn't! That's not true."

"Yes, it is."

"Who is he?"

"His name is Charles Horne, and he's with the 18th Connecticut Volunteers."

"How did you meet him?"

"His regiment was sent to Maryland to guard the canal, and the town gave a supper for the men in one of the churches. Mama and I helped serve, and that's where I met him."

"Chesapeake City gave a supper for a bunch of Yankees?" Tillman demanded, disbelieving.

"Yes. Why not? Most of us here believe in the Union cause."

"You people don't know what they're like," Tillman burst out. "They're animals!"

Sally Day was so taken aback she stared at him, speechless. The moonlight deepened the shadows on his face and turned it into a fanatical, ugly mask. Was this the gentle, merry cousin she had known in better days, in the good days before the war?

Something in her own face recalled him from his black thoughts and he took her hand and cradled it gently in his own. "Don't look so frightened, cousin," he said more reasonably. "The last thing in the world I wanted to do tonight was to frighten you. But you've got to be warned. It's absolutely out of the question for you to like one of them. I know what I'm talking about; I fought them at Gettysburg, I fought them at Fredericksburg, I was at Antietam. I know what they're like. Sally Day, they're foreigners, they're savages!"

She pulled her hand away. "I think I ought to tell you that Charles has been in southern prison camps. Two years ago he was captured and taken to Libby Prison, and later on he was sent to Belle Isle. He was exchanged and sent home to Connecticut to get his health back. He stopped to visit us. He didn't talk to me about it but he told my father how horrible those prisons were. He watched his own brother die of starvation at Belle Isle."

Sally Day shivered in her mother's warm cloak. The night was so still they heard a fish jump in the black water below. She was about to ask her cousin to take her back to the house.

Then he spoke. "I was wrong," he said dully. "War changes everybody. It brings out the best in men, but it also brings out the worst. Don't ask me to say anything good about Yankee soldiers because I can't. They've killed too many of my friends right before my eyes. But I'll grant you that when this terrible war is over and we begin to think about it, we may decide that one army wasn't any worse than the other."

His voice dropped. He said huskily, "I'm sorry I started this. I only wanted to warn you, cousin, that you mustn't let yourself love a Yankee. Even if they're no worse than we are, they're still different. You're a southern girl. Maryland's a southern state, and the fact that many good men like Uncle George have adopted the Union cause doesn't change that."

He began to plead then. "Remember before the war, when we were young? You knew I loved you. Our families have taken it for granted that we'd marry some day, that we'd spend our lives together. Please, please, cousin, don't commit yourself, don't make a promise to any soldier. I love you so much it aches inside me, but I'm not asking for your promise tonight, even when I need it so much."

Wordless, Sally Day walked beside him, trying to match the steps of her gaitered feet to his strides. They reached the wooden walk that led to the garden, and she caught his arm. "Cousin," she began.

"No," he said, "don't say anything."

"Where will you go in the morning?"

"I'm meeting a friend. A boat will take us to Virginia."

"It'll be just a short time before you'll be home again," she said, meaning to comfort him.

"It may be years," he said.

She knew better. He knew, too, that the South couldn't go on fighting very much longer, but he couldn't admit that, and she didn't want to argue. At the door, she still clung to his arm. "Come in and sleep in a real bed, Tillman. Father will wake you before daylight."

"No," he said, "The barn's safer. If the Yankees come and find me, then your parents can claim they didn't know I was anywhere around."

He unbuttoned his pocket and put a small box, wrapped in thin paper in her hand. "I bought you this in Richmond a long time ago," he said. "I've carried it everywhere with me. I lost it once on a march, but it leads a charmed life. One of our men found it in the mud and returned it to me. I planned to ask for your promise when I gave it to you, but I'm not doing that tonight. I'm giving it to you so you'll remember me, whatever happens."

The moonlight was bright enough to see by, and she started to unwrap it. "No," he said, "look at it when you're alone in your room."

He held her small face in his two hands, bent and kissed her. Then he opened the door and gave her a gentle push inside.

The children had gone to bed, but Mrs. Hammond was still sewing by the light of the lamp. "Sally Day, you've been crying," she said.

Sally Day felt her face, and it was wet. "Maybe I have, but I didn't know it."

The packet was in her hand but she didn't show it to her mother. She leaned for a moment on her shoulder. "Mama, war's a terrible thing," she whispered.

"Yes, it is, dear. I'm sorry you had to learn that so young."

Sally Day said good night, lit a candle and climbed the

stairs to her room. She opened her gift then. It was a large brooch of yellow gold, intricately carved with raised flowers, each petal and stamen clear, a beautiful and expensive thing. It was the first piece of jewelry she had ever owned.

Something made her wrap it again and hide it under the clothes in her bureau. She would take it out and look at it when she wasn't so upset.

She undressed and put on her flannel nightgown, but she didn't get into bed. Instead she folded a quilt around her and sat by the window. The barn was dark and silent.

She loved Tillman, yes, she truly did. Was it cousinly love, though, made up of memories of happy childhood times? How much play-acting was mixed up in all Tillman had said tonight? When they were children Tillman, with his vivid imagination, had been the one who had made up the games. He had carried her along into a gay, funny world he created.

She heard the back door squeak. Her parents were crossing the back yard to the barn, her father carrying a pile of quilts, her mother a basket. They were making sure that Tillman had a warm sleep and food to take on his journey.

Sally Day crouched beside the window, her head on the sill, long after her parents had returned to the house and climbed the stairs to their own room. Tears slid down her face, tears for all of them.

Tears for Tillman, facing a dangerous, lonely journey back to the Confederate Army camped somewhere in Virginia. Tears for Aunt Belle, sleeping in Chesapeake City tonight not knowing her only son was so close but didn't dare to sneak into town to see her.

Tears for everybody who was lonely, this winter night.

Tears for Charles Horne somewhere in West Virginia,

with Sheridan's army in the Shenandoah.

She finally slipped into bed, and it was Charles's dark, intense face she saw most clearly. Months had gone by since she had seen him but Charles's face was clearer than Tillman's, who had kissed her only an hour ago.

Chapter Two

FEBRUARY WAS SUPPOSED to be a short month, but to Sally Day Hammond it seemed endless. Maybe it wasn't an unusually cold, wet month in Maryland but only seemed that way. Still the days just dragged along.

She had grown up in a merry house, maybe that was the trouble. Now, in this fourth year of the War Between the States, there didn't seem to be any merriment anywhere.

Luckily her father needed help at his store, the Hammond Emporium in Chesapeake City. Every morning Sally Day bundled up warmly and climbed into the buggy with him and rode to town. After he had made up the fire in the stove, the Emporium was a pleasant place to spend the day. Few cash customers came, because not many folks had money to spend. Local people brought farm produce in and bartered with Mr. Hammond for household goods and for the staples like sugar and salt and spices, which they needed.

Sally Day stayed in the background while the bartering was going on because it wouldn't be womanly for her to join in the men's discussion, but she enjoyed it. When women came with their husbands it was Sally Day's job to help them select calico or thread or other items. Her mother had taught Sally Day to make her own clothes, and she was considered quite an authority on sewing and on style in that part of the country. Before she and her customers could get down to business they had long visits, exchanging gossip about every family in town and news of sickness and love affairs and other interesting matters.

The men joked with her. They called her Miss Short Change, because she was only five feet tall and because she was better at arithmetic than her father, and often was consulted when it came time to add up accounts.

Social life in the town was practically dead during those dark winter months. What little there was centered around Hammond's Emporium. Would the social life ever come back, Sally Day wondered. Would they ever have church socials and town dances again? Would she ever get to dance another waltz?

Her cousin Molly Gans spoke about that one day. Molly's folks lived in the back country. She and Sally Day were cousins fourth removed, but that didn't mean they weren't close kin. "Do you suppose I'll ever wear my blue challis again?" Molly asked wistfully.

"I don't know," Sally Day said. "All I do know is that mine with the pink roses is hanging on a hook in my room just gathering dust. I'm getting kind of discouraged."

"What do you hear from Mr. Horne?" Molly asked.

"I reckon he's all right. He's somewhere near Harper's Ferry, but I don't know whether there's any fighting going on around there," Sally Day told her.

Molly came around the counter. They perched on boxes, hugging themselves because they were so far from the stove. "I do think Charles Horne is the handsomest man I ever laid eyes on," Molly confided.

"Why, thank you, Molly!"

"There was one thing that struck me as odd, though," Molly went on. "When his company was stationed here, Mr. Horne came to parties but he never danced. Now wasn't that kind of odd?"

"Yes it was, and when he comes back you and I will have to teach him," Sally Day told her gaily.

"He said nobody dances where he comes from in Connecticut. What was the name of the town—Jericho? Anyway, I just can't believe that, Sally Day. Imagine! But that didn't change his being the handsomest man at any of the parties. I remember one night I sat with him and we had a right nice talk."

Molly Gans's eyes were china blue, and when she turned them on a man they could be wide with innocence. Now they were shrewd. "And what do you hear from your cousin?" she asked.

"What cousin? I've got dozens, and you know it."

"Tillman Wyatt, of course."

"I don't hear," Sally Day said. "I was planning to call on Aunt Belle soon and ask for news of him." Then she burst out, "I do wish people wouldn't talk so!"

"Why, what do you mean?"

"Some horrid person told him I'd been walking out with a Yankee soldier and Tillman was real upset—" Sally Day stopped, aghast.

Molly pounced. "How could you know that if you haven't seen Cousin Tillman?" she demanded.

Sally Day had to wiggle out of that fast. She didn't like being caught in a lie. She liked even less having Molly learn that Tillman had sneaked through the Union lines and visited the Hammond home. "All I know is the gossip, what somebody told that somebody told," she mumbled, blushing.

Luckily for her, Mrs. Gans called out then, "Where are you, Molly? It's time we thought about going home."

"I'm right here, Mama," Molly answered. She still seemed suspicious. She waited, but Sally Day kept silent.

She was longing to tell her best friend about her new gold brooch. Not another girl in the county owned such a beautiful piece of jewelry. Of course she would have to wait until the war was over before she wore it, or even told about it.

The girls kissed, and Molly promised to come soon for a week's visit at the Hammond house. Sally Day came out from behind the counter to pay her respects to Mr. and Mrs. Gans.

It was a comfort, in a way, to find out that other girls felt as she and Molly did. Lacey White Wyatt, Tillman's sister, made that clear. Although the two were first cousins they weren't exactly intimate. Lacey White was a year older than Sally Day, a serious, tall girl with deep, dark eyes. One day when she dropped in at the store to buy a spool of thread she said gloomily, "I'm seventeen and you're sixteen and we'll both be old maids before this awful war is over, Sally Day."

Sally Day drew her small face down in a vinegary look too, and agreed. She had her fingers crossed though, because she knew she wasn't going to be an old maid. How could she? She'd had two offers. It wouldn't do, though, to wave under Lacey White's nose the fact that two men had practically said right out they wanted to marry Sally Day, and one of them Lacey White's own brother!

March first finally came around. The ground turned muddy. Mr. Hammond told Sally Day she'd better stay home and help her mother, for Mrs. Hammond was beginning to think about spring housecleaning.

The two began the laborious task of cleaning the rambling, ten-room house, scrubbing, washing windows, turning out cupboards and drawers. Zeke, the town ne'er-do-well, came for a day to beat the carpets.

Wilhelmina and Eugene went to school every morning, but they were home all afternoon. Sally Day went to look for her small brother one afternoon when he was supposed to be helping Zeke clean the cellar, and found him sitting on the edge of the canal, his face in his hands, dreaming in the sun. The two hounds, Boots and Saddles, sprawled near him, sleeping. "If you've got spring fever, then I'll tell Mama to fix you a dose of sulphur and molasses," she said severely.

He wasn't listening. "The barges will start coming through soon," he said.

He loved the excitement of living near a canal. Ever since 1861, when the war began, this waterway had been busy. Besides the ordinary traffic of mule-drawn commercial boats, it had borne the barges transporting soldiers from New York to Washington.

The days when military barges went through had always been red-letter days for the three Hammond children. Their mother had fixed buckets of cooling drinks for the soldiers. The drivers had halted the mules, to let the soldiers refresh themselves.

The men had been gay and friendly, as though going off to war was an adventure. They had joked and laughed with the children, promising to bring them souvenirs of the war, praising Mrs. Hammond's cookies.

It had been far, far different when the army barges came

through later, carrying the wounded back north. The men had lain on the deck in the hot sun, frightened and often in desperate pain. Sometimes the stench had been awful. On days when a barge with wounded passed, Mrs. Hammond had never failed to go down to the canal. She went aboard with a basket full of clean cloths and helped the doctors wrap the wounded in fresh bandages. She passed among the injured men giving them cool water and fruit and soft words of comfort.

On those dreadful days Gene and Willie had stayed on shore. When Sally Day turned fifteen her mother decided she was old enough to help, and took her on board because her help was needed.

Sally Day had hated and feared those times. The suffering of the men, the sight of their terrible wounds had sickened her and she had only wanted to run and hide. But when her mother noticed this it made no difference. Sally Day hadn't been let off. Her cheerful, easy-going mother had ordered her about sharply, making her pass among the men on the deck, lifting their heads to help them drink, aiding her mother and the doctors with the dressings.

Now when Gene said, "The barges will start coming," the sun went right out of Sally Day's sky. She shivered with sudden cold. If the barges brought the wounded through, they might not all be anonymous, suffering faces. One of them could be Charles Horne. I couldn't bear it if I saw him lying there in pain, she thought.

Gene was looking up into her face curiously. The two were very close. Gene was a bright boy and guessed where her mind was wandering. "Where's Mr. Horne now?" he asked.

"He's in the Shenandoah Valley with General Sheridan."

"You're scared that he'll be shot and come on one of the

barges."

"I guess I am," Sally Day confessed. "I suppose that's what bothers me."

"He won't." Gene said positively. "He told me that he didn't intend to get killed in the war. Probably he won't even be hurt."

"It appears to me you and Corporal Horne got to be real intimate," Sally Day said lightly. She added, "Do you like him?"

"Yes, I do. I hope you'll marry him."

"Go along with you," Sally Day scoffed. "You think you're so smart and you know so much, though, maybe you can tell me something else. Do Mother and Father like him, too?"

"Yes, though I heard Mama say she wished he laughed more, that he's kind of serious for her taste."

Suddenly Gene's joy in the beginning of spring got the better of him. He let out a wild whoop and started wrestling with his boots, frantically trying to get them off. "What are you doing?" his sister demanded.

"I'm going wading. You come, too!"

"No, I'm too old for that, and Mama will scalp you if you go in the water. And we'd better get back to the house because Zeke's still waiting for you to help him clean the cellar."

Grumbling, Gene pulled his boots back on.

For the rest of that day Sally Day felt excited and nervous and didn't know why. She was expecting something to happen, and in the evening it did. When her father came home from the store he gave her a letter. "This came on the stage," he told her.

"Sally Day's heard from her beau," Gene said, grinning.

Wilhelmina tried to push her sister into a chair, begging her to open her letter. Any mail was an important event.

Mrs. Hammond rescued her. "Leave Sally Day alone and let her read her letter in peace," she ordered. "If it has things in it that will interest us, then she'll tell us about them if she wants to." Sally Day gave her a grateful look and took a candle and went up to her room to open the precious envelope.

Charles's writing was even and steady, so she knew he was in good health. There had been some fighting around Harper's Ferry, he said, but the men were full of hope that the war could not drag on much longer. He didn't say anything personal in the letter; there wasn't a single loving word. He signed himself, "Your friend, Charles Horne."

Disappointment clouded Sally Day's face. Then she thought, Maybe he just doesn't know how to write a love letter. Maybe he can't let himself go and say what he wants to. Papa says Yankees are different from southern folks.

It was Charles's silence, his reserve, his being different that had attracted Sally Day to him in the first place, she realized. They made her wonder what lay behind his dark good looks.

She brought the letter to the supper table and laid it beside her father's plate so he could read it aloud. Willy looked disappointed, too, that there weren't some romantic love words in it. "What Corporal Horne says confirms what the stage driver told me," Mr. Hammond said. "Rumor says Lee will be on the run soon and it's only a matter of weeks, perhaps only days, before the Army of the Potomac will march into Richmond.

"Mother," he addressed his wife, "the time's come. What do you say we dig up the family treasure?"

Ever since the early days of the war, what the Hammonds grandly called "the family treasure" had been buried in the back yard. Mr. Hammond was the only one who knew where it lay. Like other people of Chesapeake City they had hidden their valuables, for marauding bands had roamed the countryside. Whether they were Confederate or Union men, there had been looters ready to steal whatever they found. The war itself had come so close that more than once the Hammonds had heard artillery pounding in the distance.

Eugene ran to the barn to fetch the lantern and the family trailed Mr. Hammond outside. He led them to the end of his wife's flower border. There he dug up one of her pet white peonies and laid it aside. Not far down the spade hit something solid. Eugene scrambled into the hole and brushed the dirt away, and his father lifted out a small iron box.

Mr. Hammond staggered under its weight, while they all tried to help. Mrs. Hammond was as gay as any of the children as they gathered around the table to see the box opened.

Her own family, the Days, had once been wealthy, one of the landowning families of Maryland's eastern shore. It had fallen on hard times and both money and land had been lost. All that was left of all that wealth was the family silver, part of which had come to Mrs. Hammond as her inheritance.

This was her treasure, and it was a real one. Each piece was wrapped in oiled silk, and as her husband carefully unwrapped them and set them on the table, Willie and Eugene grew quiet, their eyes getting larger and larger.

Their mother looked as though she might cry, for after being buried in the earth for three long years her precious silver was black with tarnish. "Don't feel badly, Mama," Sally Day comforted her. "We'll clean it tomorrow, and it will be as beautiful as new."

"We won't wait until tomorrow," Mr. Hammond announced. "Your mother has a right to see how beautiful it is tonight."

They fetched cloths and the polish and sat around the table. In the soft light of the lamp the silver began to emerge in all its glory. The children polished the spoons and silver buckles and small pieces, Sally Day worked on the massive tray, her father did the creamers and sugar bowls and the half-dozen solid-silver plates. Mrs. Hammond tenderly shined the loveliest things of all, the two large, ornate teapots.

When they were finished and the pieces had been washed in soapy water and buffed to make them shine, the younger children stared at the display with dazzled eyes. "My goodness, Mama," Sally Day said with a choke in her voice, "I'd kind of forgotten we were so rich."

Her mother looked around the circle of faces. She said contentedly, "I hadn't forgotten, for it isn't silver that makes a family rich, it's love and kindness to each other." Then her joyous laugh rang out and she cried, "Oh, my darlings, we're the luckiest folks on earth. The war's almost over, peace is almost here. Let's smash that awful brown teapot we've been using! From now on we'll drink like lords and ladies out of silver again!"

Chapter Three

WHEN IMPORTANT NEWS was sent out from Washington it came by telegraph to Elkton, Maryland, and from there it traveled by stagecoach to Chesapeake City. The natural place for the daily stage to stop was in front of Hammond's Emporium. Thus, George Hammond was usually the first person to learn of any great event.

On April 5 of that spring of 1865 he came home to supper bearing the news that Petersburg, Virginia, had been taken by the Union forces. "How long can Richmond hold out, then?" his wife asked.

"Not long," he assured her.

The following afternoon Josiah Buggles, who worked at the Emporium, came whooping along the road on Mr. Hammond's horse. Sally Day and Gene and Willie tumbled out of the house to learn what his hollering was about. "Richmond's fallen!" he yelled.

Mr. Hammond confirmed this when he came home that evening. He had sent Josiah to ride through town calling the good news.

The next day it seemed as though time stood still. That spring had been particularly beautiful so far. One bright, blue day followed another. Forsythia sprawled everywhere in showers of gold. "It appears like Nature's pleased, too, that the end has come," Mrs. Hammond said contentedly.

A barge hove into sight on the canal that afternoon, carrying a load of new recruits for the Union Army. Gene Hammond rushed through the garden to call out to them, "You'll never get to fight, the war's almost over!" The men on deck sent up a thunderous cheer. They called down to Gene, that he was a fine, brave young man, and asked why he didn't come along with them to see the Rebs on the run and the end of the war. Sally Day and Willie seized their brother's jacket to hold him back, and then the men cheered them, too, and one called, "If all the girls in Maryland are as pretty as you, then we'll never go back home again!"

When the final news came through that General Lee had met General Grant at Appomattox and that the peace had been signed, there was little celebrating. Mr. Hammond closed the store and hurried home to tell his wife. He put his arms around her and they both wept. The children stared at their mother and father uncertainly. Eugene rushed into the house whooping, and Sally Day seized him and put her hand over his mouth.

Their parents opened their arms to take all the children in, and Mr. Hammond started the Doxology and they sang together, "Praise God from Whom All Blessings Flow." Everyone cried, and for the rest of that day they moved quietly, so full of thankfulness that four hard, ugly, bitter years of war were over, their hearts were overflowing.

Mrs. Hammond put their feeling into words. "Now we know that no more young men are going to die," she said. "People can stop hating each other. Oh, that must make Mr. Lincoln very happy!"

Sally Day guessed that everyone was thinking of the tall, gaunt man in the White House, and how the victory must have eased his sore heart. She shared in the general rejoicing and went with her mother to the church, to join in planning a big homecoming celebration for the town's own soldiers.

But for her own part, she had trouble keeping her thoughts on quite so high a plane as her elders did. Molly Gans was at the meeting, too, and the girls fell into each other's arms. "Now maybe we'll begin to have some fun again," Molly said. "I hope there'll be a lot of parties, to make up for lost time."

The older women were debating whether they should give a dinner for the whole town when the boys returned. Many, like Mrs. Hammond, wanted to welcome back the veterans of the defeated southern armies, too, so that the bitterness that had divided the town would begin to heal. Tired of the discussion, Sally Day and Molly wandered outside, and Lacey White joined them.

A bush of bridal wreath grew by the church steps, and Molly broke off a sprig of white blossoms and arched it over Sally Day's head. The petals drifted off and mixed with Sally Day's smooth, dark hair, and laughing she brushed them away. "We've got one party to look forward to, anyway," Molly said, "and that's Sally Day's wedding."

"Sally Day's and who's wedding?" Lacey White demanded sharply.

Molly remembered too late that Lacey White would be shocked to learn Sally Day was thinking seriously of marrying a Yankee. "Oh, it seems to me there was one soldier who was kind of smitten with her, but I was only teasing," she said lamely.

"Sally Day, you wouldn't marry that terrible man from Connecticut. I don't believe it!"

Sally Day couldn't let that pass. Bearing in mind how Lacey White's family must feel now that the South had lost, she said gently, "I'm not planning to marry anybody right away, Lacey White, but I wish you wouldn't call Corporal Horne a terrible man, because he's really very nice."

Lacey White drew herself up to her considerable height. "Have you forgotten so soon that my own brother, who's your first cousin, fought with Lee?"

Molly broke in, "Oh, Lacey White, let's not fight that old war again! It's over, and everything's changed. It's a lovely world we live in, so let's forget the bad times. Let's only think of the good times ahead."

The girls were unaware that the minister was standing at the top of the church steps. Now he came down to join them. He had fought in the war and lost an arm at Shiloh, and since then he hadn't had an easy time trying to minister to a congregation that was half Union, half Confederate. He said now, "That was good advice, Molly. Girls like you three who are kin were never really enemies. It's not just your Christian duty to forget your differences, it's good common sense, as Molly pointed out."

"What are the ladies doing inside?" Sally Day asked.

"They're still talking, but they've decided to put off their celebration until a little time has gone by. Later on, Maryland folks will be more ready to meet together like old friends and neighbors. I believe it was a wise decision."

Molly made a face. "I don't," she said. "That just means we're cheated out of a party." The minister chuckled.

Without any parties, though, those April days were still like a celebration. The sun lay softly on the spring-fresh earth. Leaves were unfurling in new greens, flowers were popping up. Everyone was waiting for the boys to come drifting back home, waiting to see what Mr. Lincoln was going to do about the South, now that he was President of the whole country again.

On the fifteenth of April Sally Day went to town with her father. A rain the night before had turned the road to brown mush, and Chesapeake City's main street was a quagmire. The mud spattered up from the buggy's wheels, soiling the hem of Sally Day's calico gown. When her father stopped in front of the Emporium he had to drive some pigs away so he could help her down to the granite horse block.

It was strange how that moment printed itself on Sally Day's mind, to stay with her forever. Her father had just turned and raised his arms to lift her down when Josiah burst out the door. "Mr. Hammond, there's terrible news! Mr. Lincoln's been shot!" he called.

Mr. Hammond set Sally Day down on the porch of the Emporium and said, "Josh, your brains must be addled to say such a thing." Then they saw a group of men running up the street, and their faces showed that Josh's story was true.

They all went inside the store. Mr. Hammond had to hear the stage driver tell the news himself before he could believe it. The driver repeated that word had come over the telegraph to Elkton that the President had been shot the evening before at Ford's Theatre in Washington.

"But he's not dead," someone said.

The stage driver said in a dull voice, "I may have been too upset to get it straight, but the way I understand it he was shot while he sat with Mrs. Lincoln watching the play, and the bullet went into his head."

Sally Day let out a cry of fright and sudden grief. "Stop that!" her father ordered sharply.

They had all been standing around as though they were in a trance. Sally Day's cry seemed to recall them to themselves. Mr. Smithton, who kept the town stable, said, "You'd better take your daughter home, George. The town will be no place for womenfolk today."

Mr. Hammond turned to him. "What do you mean?"

Mr. Smithton's face flamed turkey red and he said, "Some Secesh did this damnable thing to the President. There'll be fighting in the street if any of them show their faces."

"Mr. Smithton's right," Mr. Hammond said then. "Sally Day, I'll drive you home."

Her face was wet with tears and she didn't care who saw. She begged, "Papa, please let me stay, I'll be quiet."

"No," her father said. There was no arguing with that firm "no."

He held the door for her. They stepped outside, and saw a stranger tying his horse at the rail. The look on his face was awful. He suddenly sobbed, and Mr. Hammond ordered, "Speak, man!" The men poured out of the store and others came running, aware that something momentous was happening.

The stranger pulled himself together, drew in his breath. He said, "The news came to Elkton that Mr. Lincoln died at eight o'clock this morning. An actor by the name of John Wilkes Booth shot him. Another assassin tried to kill Mr. Seward, the Secretary of State. They don't know whether General Grant is alive. He'd left Washington but they think he was marked for death, too. The actor Booth hasn't been caught and he may be headed this way."

Sally Day heard one man cursing, but the faces of most were pale and stony. Her father helped her into the buggy and they drove home in silence. She couldn't stop crying, and as they neared home her father said, "Your tears do you credit, daughter, but now wipe your face. Your mother will think we've suffered some personal tragedy if she sees you so."

She did as she was told. Her father added, "This is a personal tragedy, though, for every American."

"Not for the Secesh!" Sally Day cried.

"For them perhaps most of all. They needed Mr. Lincoln's wisdom and humanity even more than the rest of us."

Mrs. Hammond guessed that something was wrong when she saw the buggy at the gate. Mr. Hammond called Wilhelmina and Eugene from the barn and told them all the terrible news. Then he went back to town.

The children stayed close to their mother, their faces full of questions. Eugene looked scared, but Willie was a spit-fire and she cried, "If I got hold of that assassin I'd kill him with my own hands!"

"Don't talk foolishness!" her mother snapped. Then she said more gently, "We'll all keep busy, and then even if we can't put this awful thing out of our minds we'll be better off. Sally Day, string a line between the apple trees and carry out the quilts and air them. Willie will help you. Gene, I want you to go along the canal and dig me a mess of dandelion greens for supper."

While her little sister gathered up all the quilts in the house, Sally Day found a piece of clothesline and tied it between two apple trees. Willie came across the grass carrying her first load. Sally Day said, "Listen."

Willie did for a minute, then said, "I don't hear anything."

"That's what I mean," Sally Day said. "It's so quiet."

Even the birds, busy with nest building in the maples, sounded muted. Not a voice was carried on the air, not a dog barked. The silence was brooding and ominous, the air heavy, the way it was sometimes when clouds were piling up before the thunder cracked. "I wonder if it's this way everywhere," Willie said, her brown eyes big with awe.

"Probably everywhere in the whole world people would hold their breath if they knew the President of the United States has been killed," Sally Day said slowly.

Chapter Four

THEY MOVED THROUGH the next day carefully. It occurred to Sally Day that each person acted as if he were a piece of brittle glass, and it would take only a slight jar to break him. Once Willie and Gene started wrangling over a kitten, and Mrs. Hammond sobbed, "Children, how can you at a time like this?"

Every traveler through town brought word of how the search for John Wilkes Booth was going. News came that several people had been arrested and accused of being in the plot with Booth. Once a troop of Union cavalry came tearing along the road, thundering past the Hammond gate. The children believed they were on Booth's trail.

Mr. Hammond was absolutely determined that the whole family was going to see the President. His wife protested, "George, that is folly. The country is in a terrible state and it isn't safe to travel. We can honor Lincoln with our prayers."

For once her husband wouldn't listen to her. "We never saw him alive but we are going to see him in his coffin. All their lives the children will remember it, Sarah. They must remember. I don't care what lengths we have to go to, how hard the journey is, we will make it."

His wife opened her mouth to speak but he said, "We are going to Mr. Lincoln's funeral," in a voice that left no room for argument.

He took the stage to Elkton, to learn how best to get to Washington. He came home to report that he'd been advised not to try it, that people were pouring into the capital from all over the country. After the funeral, however, the President's body was to travel by train to Illinois, his home state, and the funeral train would stop at many large cities so the people could pay honor to him. Baltimore, Maryland, was to be the first stop on this sad journey. The Hammonds would go to Baltimore to pay their respects.

Thus it was that on April 20 the Hammond family boarded the Baltimore train at Elkton. To Mrs. Hammond's question about whether they could afford to spend a night at a hotel, her husband answered that the cost didn't matter. They had to be in Baltimore the following morning when the funeral train arrived.

The children had never spent a night at a hotel before, and Willie and Gene were bursting with excitement. Sally Day warned them with scowls and whispers that they were to behave and not disturb their father. His face quite awed her, for it was stiff with grief.

The railroad station in Baltimore, the hotel, most of the buildings were draped in mourning black. A weird quiet hung over the streets and people spoke in whispers. The Hammonds had taken two rooms, and gathered in a front window that looked down on the main street. "They all love Lincoln here now," Mrs. Hammond said sadly, watching how quietly the people moved. Even the hooves of the carriage horses sounded muffled.

"Why Mama, what do you mean?" Sally Day exclaimed.

"Everybody always loved the President!"

"You've forgotten, or else you never knew," her father said. "When Mr. Lincoln called up the first troops four years ago, mobs rioted against them here in Baltimore. The people threw paving stones, then fired on the troops, and several were killed. They disliked the President here particularly, but he had enemies everywhere in the North." Mr. Hammond finished bitterly, "Now when it's too late they'll claim they always loved and admired him."

Showers that began during the night turned into a steady rain when dawn broke the next morning. Sally Day had slept fitfully on a cot a maid had put up in her parents' room. After all sounds ceased in the street below, the silence had seemed ominous. Mr. Hammond awakened the children early and led them down to breakfast in the hotel dining room.

They ate hurriedly and went outside. Despite the rain, crowds were gathering, pressing toward the railroad station. Mrs. Hammond hung back, and Sally Day saw that she, too, was afraid. The Hammonds were country people, and the city frightened them. Her husband said, "We'll take hands, and not let go of each other."

When they stepped into the street the crowd absorbed them. Mr. Hammond led, then Sally Day, Willie and Gene, with Mrs. Hammond at the end of the chain. Sally Day's trouble was her height, so that her father's broad back was all she could see. Willie clutched her hand so tightly it ached. Because of the rain she couldn't tell whether it was rain or tears that wet the thousands of faces in the throng.

Mr. Hammond muttered desperately, "We must see, we must." He succeeded in pulling them free of the swarms of people and they found places in the crowd lining the tracks.

They were only twenty feet away from the rails when the train bearing the President steamed slowly around a curve.

The engine looked oddly gay, for flags flew from both sides of it. Then the car came in sight, draped in black. The train jarred to a stop. A stately black hearse drew up, its black horses sleek, wet with rain. Rain was beginning to wilt the hearse's velvet draping and heavy plumes.

The coffin appeared, and a great sigh went up from the people. The pale face of a woman showed at a window of the train. Mrs. Hammond whispered, "That must be Mrs. Lincoln. Oh, the poor woman."

Behind them somebody said, "She's doubly sad today, for she's taking the coffin of her little boy back to Illinois."

Mrs. Hammond asked, "Which son was that?"

"It was her son Willie, who died in the White House."

Maybe Wilhelmina Hammond was too young to know about that tragedy. Now she let out a loud wail. "His name was Willie, too!"

Sally Day ordered sharply, "Keep quiet!" Then she realized that Wilhelmina's grief was real, that her little sister was terrified and on the edge of panic. It occurred to her, Maybe Papa was wrong to expose the children to anything like this. She drew Willie to her and held her tenderly and tightly.

The coffin was carefully and reverently carried to the hearse. Thousands of people turned and moved after it. Nobody pushed or acted rough. They walked so solemnly and silently, the clop, clop of the hooves striking the cobblestones could be distinctly heard. Sally Day realized, As long as I live I'll never hear that sound without remembering today. Bells tolled. At regular intervals guns were firing.

The thousands paused as the coffin was carried into the

Exchange Building. Police moved among them, directing them into lines, four abreast. Sally Day held Willie's hand and her parents took Gene. For an hour they stood patiently while the rain penetrated their clothes to the skin. Willie shivered constantly but did not complain. At last their turn came. They mounted the steps and entered the rotunda.

The lines, four people wide, slowly circled the hall, where the open coffin stood on a catafalque. Sally Day caught the scent of roses, of magnolias. Their group edged closer. Willie's small face was fearful as she asked Sally Day, "Are you going to look?"

"Yes," Sally Day said. "You must, too, darling, even if you don't want to, for if you don't you'll be sorry to the last day you live,"

They neared the long coffin that was covered with black cloth. Its massive silver handles gleamed in the pale light of that dreary day. They were so close, Sally Day could read the inscription on the silver plate,

Abraham Lincoln
Sixteenth President of the United States
Born February 12, 1809
Died April 15, 1865

Just ahead of Sally Day and Willie, a Negro woman broke loose from the crowd. A soldier quickly came forward to push her back in line. She was carrying a limp bunch of violets in her trembling hand, and she begged, "Please let me give these to Mr. Lincoln!"

An officer took her by the arm and led her to the coffin, and helped her lay her flowers inside.

Sally Day's throat ached with unshed tears, but she was determined not to cry. She realized confusedly, This is part of growing up, learning to face things. I must act grown up for Willie's sake. We've both got to look at him.

It wasn't as hard as she had feared. She thought she knew the President's face, for she had seen it often in pictures. She expected it to be gaunt and homely, with deep-sunk eyes and grief-carved lines, and a big, ugly mole. Now she was astonished to see how beautiful Mr. Lincoln's face was. His head rested against a white silk pillow. She stared at him as long as she could, until the crowd pushed her on. She thought numbly, I've got to carry this picture with me, because then maybe I'll understand him. Yes, she understood a little now, for she had been able to read the loving kindness in that still face.

The throng carried them through the door, and they made their way back to the railroad station. The rain hadn't let up but it didn't matter, for they couldn't get any wetter than they were. The lines waiting to get into the Exchange Building extended all the way to the station. The Hammonds walked along it, and every once in awhile someone in the line asked, "Did you see him?"

"Yes," Mr. Hammond answered.

"How did he look?"

"Beautiful," Mr. Hammond said, and that would have been Sally Day's answer, too.

They found seats in the station, and it was warm and dry. They had no idea how long they would have to wait for a train to take them to Elkton. They were still waiting hours later, when the funeral cortege again passed through the streets, the church bells mournfully tolling, the cannon booming. They watched the coffin being reverently put aboard its car, watched the black-draped train move slowly down the tracks on the way to Philadelphia, the next stage of its sad journey.

They were too full of emotion to talk. At last the train for Elkton was announced, and people jostled to get aboard. Mr. Hammond led his little flock through the cars vainly looking for seats. His wife was drooping with exhaustion and a soldier in Union blue got up and offered her his place.

She argued, feeling that no civilian ought to take a seat away from a soldier, but he insisted, "Please, ma'am, I'd be honored." She thanked him and took Gene on her lap. The little boy was soon asleep on her shoulder.

Sally Day and Willie clung to their father, swaying with the motion of the train, half asleep with weariness. Dusk came as they watched the Maryland countryside flow by. The rain stopped, and the sun broke through the low clouds.

They were almost into Elkton when Gene stirred heavily, sat up straight and let out a sobbing yell. "Gene, be quiet," his father ordered.

But he continued to sob. Sally Day thought perhaps she could help him, and leaned down and said, "Gene, we all feel terrible about the President, but you must stop your grieving for you'll only make yourself sick."

Gene looked up at her, his eyes brimming, and said, "I'm not crying for the President, I'm hungry! I haven't had any-thing to eat since breakfast!"

The soldier who had given Mrs. Hammond his place smiled, and then laughter ran through the railroad car. Sally Day was ashamed for him, but she saw that her father's grim face had relaxed.

He tapped Gene on the shoulder. "Don't mind folks laughing, son," he said. "Maybe we needed something to lighten our spirits. I'm sorry I forgot to feed you, but we'll be home soon."

They slept on the jolting ride in the stage, home to Chesapeake City. Their own buggy was still tied to the rail in front of the Emporium, and poor old Major, who had stood all day in the pouring rain, wheezed a welcome when he saw them coming.

A lamp was lit in the store, and Josiah Buggles was waiting. Gene made straight for the barrel of crackers and stuffed his mouth full. "How was the funeral?" Josiah asked.

"I'll tell you about it in the morning," his boss promised.

"The stage came through with the mail."

"I'll sort the mail in the morning, too," Mr. Hammond said. "Right now I've got to get my family home."

Josh was an admirer of Sally Day's, and now he looked at her in a way that always made her furious. "I took the liberty of sorting out a letter of Miss Sally's," he said, and gave it to her.

"Get in the buggy," Mr. Hammond ordered. "You can read your letter when we get home, Sally Day."

Josh hadn't finished with his news. "Miss Sally, your soldier feller is coming next week," he announced. "The letter came unstuck so I took the liberty of reading it, to see if there was anything important. Corporal Horne, isn't he your soldier feller?"

Really angry now, Sally Day opened her mouth to tell him off. Her mother said wearily, "Come along, Sally Day. I know you want to scold Josiah and he did do wrong, but we've got to get these children home and put them to bed. One way or another, we've got to put an end to this long, long day."

Chapter Five

INDEED CORPORAL HORNE'S letter was important, for he wrote that he expected to be mustered out of the army any day. He reported that his company had heard the sad news from Washington. "Oh, what a dark pall fell over the Army to think that our beloved President is dead," he wrote.

He went on to tell her that if the 18th Regiment was mustered out at Harper's Ferry then he would go straight to Chesapeake City. If the men had to travel to Connecticut to be released, then he would come south as soon as he could.

There was a determined tone in his letter that made Sally Day's heart beat faster. Her parents were in their bedroom when she sought them out to read it to them. "Are you upset, darling?" her mother asked.

"I don't know, Mama. Maybe I am," Sally Day confessed.

"It's quite clear you're either going to have to fish or cut bait, daughter," her father said with a wry smile. "This Yankee doesn't sound like one of our boys that any smart southern girl can dangle on her string."

Sally Day kissed her parents and went to her own room. She thought, Papa's right, Charles wouldn't understand flirting. She remembered the expression on his intent, brooding face once when she had kissed him lightly and then laughed and said it didn't mean anything. She had complained, "Don't look at me that way, Charles. I feel like a butterfly stuck on a pin."

"That's what you are, a butterfly," he had said angrily.

Did she really love him? she wondered. Well, when she daydreamed about boys and about being married someday, it was Corporal Horne she thought of, wasn't it? Wasn't it his face that swam before her eyes, when she couldn't sleep and lay wakeful in her bed?

She had never shown her parents the gold brooch Tillman had given her, and now she wished she had. Accepting it might take some explaining. She was too worn out by the long, terrible day to think clearly. She lay with her arms under her head, staring into the darkness. Somewhere outside in the dark, sleepy doves were murmuring. I've got to tell Mama and Papa how I felt about Tillman, too, she thought, but how can I when I don't know myself?

She and Molly had decided that the end of the war meant the beginning of good times, of parties and light-hearted gaiety. Well, she knew that the terrible death of the President had put an end to anything like that for awhile. Now Corporal Horne's letter was a warning that Sally Day had better begin to think seriously about her future.

The next morning she called her mother into her room and showed her the brooch. Mrs. Hammond didn't reproach her for not showing it before. "A girl's got a right to her own secrets," she said. "It's a beautiful thing, a costly thing."

"Does Aunt Belle have a lot of money? Could Tillman afford it?"

"Oh, yes. There's no money problem in that branch of the family. Now that you've shown it to me, tell me the truth, Sally Day. Is it an engagement gift?"

"Oh, no, Mama!"

"You didn't make any promises to Tillman?"

"No. It was just a cousinly sort of a present, I'm sure of that."

"I'm not so sure," her mother said, troubled. "Sally Day, I think you're going to have to make up your mind how you feel about your cousin before Mr. Horne comes. Of course we're not talking about marriage. Why, you're just a little girl. It'll be years before you'll be thinking about that."

"How old were you when you married Papa?" Sally Day knew the answer, but she wanted to hear her mother say it.

Mrs. Hammond gave her a sharp look, then laughed. "You think you caught me, child. Yes, I was only sixteen, too, but I was a much older sixteen than you are."

"I don't know whether that's exactly so or not," Sally Day said slowly. "It seems like we all grew up early during these last four years. Molly Gans says we never had our playtime, and she's right."

Her mother gave her back the pin. "We'll talk again any time you want to, dear."

"Can I wear it? It'll look lovely on my wool delaine."

"I don't think you should. It looks too elegant to be a cousinly kind of gift."

"Tillman put it in my hand and didn't let me see it, that night he slept in our barn. I'm very sure it didn't mean anything serious to him. Oh, Mama, you know Tillman. He's not an old sober-sides, he wasn't expecting a promise."

The next afternoon she was in the back yard spreading sheets to bleach in the sun, when a horse came jogging along the road. She shielded her eyes against the sun's glare, and noted that the man wore blue and that the horse was a dusty, homely old nag. She slipped behind a tree. The rider didn't see her and she watched him stop at the gate and tie his horse to the post. He moved slowly as though he was sick or in pain.

Somehow she had half-doubted that Charles Horne was real. He was a brave soldier who was fighting for his country, who had walked out with her a few times. But he was like a romantic hero, not an actual man.

He came up the walk slowly and went around to the side door.

Soon Mrs. Hammond called from the back porch, "Sally Day!"

"Coming, Mama." She gathered up an armful of linen and crossed the grass. He was waiting inside the door. She put down her burden.

"Hello, Mr. Horne," she said.

He took her hand and clung to it as though he couldn't let it go. His face was rough with black stubble, for he needed a shave. His eyes glowed. He looks awful but I surely forgot how handsome he is, Sally Day thought, confused because her mother was watching.

"Take the young man out in the yard where it's cool, and I'll bring him something to eat," Mrs. Hammond directed, smiling. She didn't say "your young man." Sally Day couldn't guess how her mother really felt about this boy from Connecticut. However, rules of Maryland hospitality were so strict that any acquaintance had to be welcomed graciously and given shelter as long as he cared to stay.

Charles slumped on the bench under the apple tree. He said heavily, "I'm sorry I've come in such condition, Sally

Day. I haven't slept for three nights. I walked one whole day, then traded my watch for that poor beast at your gate. I'll have to take care of him."

He started to get up, but Sally Day pushed him down on the bench. "No, my brother will put him in the barn and feed him."

Gene was fishing from the bank of the canal. Sally Day ran to the bottom of the garden and hollered to him. When she rejoined Charles, Mrs. Hammond was spreading a napkin on the bench, setting out a meal of cold fried chicken and hominy cakes and milk. "Goodness, Mama, I thought Mr. Horne might collapse before you got here with the food," Sally Day giggled nervously.

Charles picked up a piece of chicken, but his hand shook so he had to put it down. Mrs. Hammond took command then. She said quietly, "Mr. Horne, you're not just tired, you're ill."

He drew a long breath before he answered. "Maybe you're right, ma'am. I'm sorry, I shouldn't have come. I wanted to see your daughter the worst way, that's my excuse."

"Are you wounded?"

"No, ma'am, not recently. I took a minie ball in my shoulder at Cedar Creek last fall, and after that came down with a fever. The last two nights, sleeping out, the fever came back on me."

"You never wrote you were wounded," Sally Day said, beginning to cry.

Gene came running up the path to meet Charles. He worshipped all soldiers who wore the Union blue. His mother put out a hand to stop him. "Gene, go take care of the horse. Sally Day, take Mr. Horne's other arm and we'll get him into the house."

Charles was still protesting as they helped him in. "Ma'am, let me go. I don't want to put you to trouble, and I'll find a room in the town."

Mrs. Hammond's tone was unusually sharp, for her. "Our home is yours, and it's an honor to our house to have a good soldier as our guest, so we'll say no more about leaving."

They steadied him up the stairs, and Sally Day ran ahead to turn down the covers of the guest-room bed. They laid him down. His head fell back on the pillow and his eyes closed. Mrs. Hammond took one boot and Sally Day the other and they wrestled them off. Then they covered him up. "Heat some water and bring me soap and cloths," Mrs. Hammond ordered.

Sally Day brought the things her mother had asked for. Charles slept heavily, his face ashen pale under his stubble of beard. Mrs. Hammond had pulled off his heavy jacket and his shirt. His shoulder was exposed, showing an ugly, colored, puckered wound. "Oh Mama, is he going to die?" Sally Day cried.

"No, of course not. This old wound never healed properly and it's sloughing some. We'll take care of that. I'm ashamed for the Union doctors that they let him get into such a state, then sent him off to fight when he should have been in a hospital."

She ordered Sally Day out then. Sally Day huddled on the stairs, and Willie and Gene joined her. Their mother gave Charles a bath, then roused him awake and made him drink a potion she had mixed to cool his fever.

She waited for her husband to come before she started to work on the shoulder wound. Through the open door, Sally Day heard her father say, "Thank God he made it. He might have died on the road."

"He really loves our daughter," Mrs. Hammond mur-mured.

Charles let out one terrible cry, when they began to dress the wound. Mr. Hammond fetched the whiskey bottle he kept for emergencies, and forced him to take a dram. Sally Day guessed that he tried to refuse it. He had told her once that his family were all teetotalers, believing that drink was the tool of the devil. After that Charles let her parents work, and only ground his teeth and muttered.

Two days passed before Sally Day saw him again. She and the children were kept out of the room, her father stayed home and he and his wife nursed Charles night and day. There was no doctor nearer than Elkton, and Mrs. Hammond considered him such an ignorant old fool she felt she could handle the emergency better herself in view of her proven skill and experience.

On the third day her mother told her, "You can sit by him while I sleep, Sally Day. I confess I'm just about done in. Get him to take some soup. Maybe he'll drink it for you. Call me if his face feels hotter. Don't be afraid, child, he isn't going to die, although he does look rather terrible."

Charles slept heavily. With several days' whiskers and with his dark coloring, he looked unkempt and wild. Nevertheless, when Wilhelmina stuck her head in and saw her sister fanning him, she whispered, awestruck, "Sally Day, you look just like a real nurse who is succoring a brave hero fallen on the battlefield."

"Shhh, go along with you," Sally Day ordered. She was pleased by the picture her sister had seen, however. She did enjoy the feeling of being a heroine cooling the soldier's fevered brow and nursing him back to health.

Charles stirred and opened his eyes, saw her and reached

for her hand. She let him keep it when he slept again, although her back got to aching from sitting still so long.

That evening her father shaved the sick man, and after that Charles looked pale and interesting and not so wild. Sally Day wished Molly would drop in and happen on the charming scene. Not another girl in Chesapeake City had a real, live but wounded soldier to care for.

His shoulder healed well, and in a few days he was sitting up and apologizing for causing the Hammonds so much trouble. Willie and Gene became his devoted slaves, smothering him with attention. Soon he was able to totter out of doors, and sat under the apple tree with a blanket over his knees.

Willie took Sally Day aside. "Now you're going to have to marry him," she informed her.

"I don't have to marry anyone," Sally Day contradicted.

"Oh, yes, you do. The story would come out all wrong if you didn't."

"This isn't a story, it's real," Sally Day corrected her. In her heart, though, she agreed with Willie. It would be a real shame if the story didn't come out right.

Charles didn't seem to understand about Maryland hospitality, and fretted because his visit had lasted two weeks. One evening when they were all sitting out after supper, watching a sickle moon climb the sky, he told the Hammonds he was leaving for Jericho the next day.

The suddenness of his announcement caught Sally Day unawares. First she was hurt and then she was mad. Her father and mother and the children started urging Charles to stay anther week anyway. Sally Day kept silent.

He had lived under her roof for two weeks and hadn't uttered one single word of love. He hadn't begged her for one single kiss. All Sally Day could conclude was that he found her displeasing now, or else that he had never been serious.

Not only was she angry, she was dismayed. What if it got around the town that Sally Day's soldier had let her nurse him back to health and then had gone off without declaring himself? Sally Day thought she'd never be able to hold up her head again.

Charles interrupted her musings. "Sally Day, will you leave us, please?"

She said defiantly, "Why should I?"

"I asked you please to leave us," he said in a softer voice.

She felt like saying, "No, I won't." Instead she got up and started for the house, astonished to find herself obeying him.

"Willie and Gene, you go along, too," Mrs. Hammond ordered.

There wasn't any lamp in the kitchen, and Willie and Gene hung out of the window straining their ears to hear what was being discussed under the apple tree. Sally Day said, "You ought to be ashamed to listen where you're not wanted."

"You know perfectly well he's out there asking for your hand in marriage," Willie said rapturously.

"I don't know any such thing, and even if he is, I don't have the least intention of accepting him. Why, I don't know him in the first place, and his manners are awful and he's really very uncouth, he's not a gentleman at all—"

"Sally Day, you can come now," Mr. Hammond called.

She stopped to tidy her hair, and Willie got behind her and pushed her out the door.

"Sally Day, Corporal Horne has asked for your hand in marriage," Mr. Hammond said. "I've told him that you're too young to think of such a serious thing, but your mother and I have given our consent for him to speak to you."

Charles stood up. She could see his pale face in the dark. He didn't touch her, but stood five feet away from her and said, "Sally Day, will you marry me?"

Sally Day forgot that she couldn't stand him and that he was a boor, and an uncouth one at that, and stammered, "Why, yes. Corporal Horne, I think I'd like to."

Chapter Six

EVEN THOUGH SALLY Day had just consented to become his wife, Charles left for the North the next day.

Sally Day begged him to stay. She was feeling solemn, and proud of the honor he had done her. Perhaps she didn't know him too well, but she was sure of one thing, that he wouldn't give his heart lightly.

Besides, she wanted to show him off. He was a handsome, pale and interesting hero, and she would have liked to take him on a round of calls to all her relatives.

This last was a petty, niggling kind of a reason, and she knew it. She was trying to learn from her parents how to be honest with herself. She even confessed it to Charles.

They walked along the canal the morning he left, their hands intertwined. "You're not well enough to ride to Connecticut," she protested. "I'll worry about you every step of the way. If you'll stay another week then you'll be stronger, and we'll have a lovely time. All my aunts and uncles and cousins will want to meet you and entertain you. There won't be big parties because of what happened to poor Mr. Lincoln, and besides, there are too many Secesh boys coming home, and it would be kind of rude to have parties and not invite the Secesh families—"

Charles stopped her chatter by swinging her around so he could look into her face. He towered over her by a foot, and it always thrilled her to the marrow of her bones when he leaned down, bending that dark, intent look on her. "Sally Day, you think too much about parties," he admonished her gently.

"No, I don't!" she exclaimed. Then, "Do I?"

"Yes, I'm afraid you do. When you come home with me to Jericho to live, you'll find it very different. We don't think about social affairs so much, the way you do. And there are some of your relatives I wouldn't care to meet."

A grim look had settled on his face and Sally Day said, "Oh, Charles, forgive me! For a moment I let myself forget about all the fighting, and your brother who died."

Charles said, "I don't ask you to hate your blood kin, because they fought against the Union."

"And I haven't any right to expect you to like them," Sally Day said earnestly. "Charles, I reckon I'm a scatterbrain and I'm just so glad the horrid war is over and you came back safely, I want to think it never happened."

"It will take time to heal the wounds," Charles said heavily. "My parents are bitter, and can't help it. My brother shouldn't have starved in that camp. It was a useless and senseless death. It's because Ben's gone that we'll make our home with my people. Father needs my help on the farm."

"Oh, I wish I could go with you now!" Sally Day mourned. "Charles, Papa listens to you. Please talk to him. It's so silly for us to wait until fall! We could be married quietly, with no fuss, and then I could go home with you, and I'd love your mother to pieces, and help her, and maybe she wouldn't miss your brother quite so much if she had a new daughter in the house."

Sally Day was getting all worked up with enthusiasm at this prospect, and her fiancé stopped her with a gentle shake. "No, Sally Day. Your father and I know best what's right to do."

Charles's strength was one of the things Sally Day loved about him. She said meekly, "Very well, Charles."

He hesitated before he went on. "Perhaps I ought to warn you that Connecticut people aren't exactly like you Maryland folks. It'll take them a little time for them to get to know you, and for you to know them. I wrote my parents that I intended to marry a southern girl, and they'll have to get used to that idea—"

Sally Day interrupted fervently, "Oh, Charles, I think from the very beginning you intended to marry me! You were going to sweep me off my feet!"

He looked startled and then he picked her up and swung her by her elbows. "It's as easy to sweep you off your feet as it would be a kitten. You don't weigh a hundred pounds."

"I do, too, I weigh exactly a hundred pounds. One day at the store Father put me on the scales with a hundred-pound bag of seed corn and we weighed exactly the same."

They turned and started slowly for home. It seemed very, very hard for Charles to make any remark that was intimate and affectionate. Sally Day guessed he cared for her deeply, and yet so far he hadn't said, "I love you," the three words that came so easily to her own lips. Now he was struggling with some thought. Finally he said gruffly, "You're good for me, you make me laugh. You'll be good for us on the farm."

She got him to talking about the Horne farm then. He did make it sound beautiful. He told her that when he and

his brother were growing up they had been told that each
would receive two hundred acres of land when he married.
Charles warned her though that they wouldn't be able to
build their own home right away. They would live in the
main farmhouse with his parents until Charles had saved
up the money to build.

Sally Day tried to tell him her own father might loan
them the money for that, but Charles said, "No." She didn't
argue. Her lover's no sounded very final.

He put on the uniform she had washed and pressed. She
hated to let him go, and begged to ride behind him on his
horse for a while, but again Charles said no. He thanked
the Hammonds for their kindness and respectfully said
goodbye to them. He carefully kissed Sally Day, and left
her swinging on the gate with Willie and Gene, who gazed
after him with worshipping eyes as he rode off, sitting tall
in the saddle.

Sally Day ran to the barn where she could be alone to
cry. She skimmed up the ladder to the loft, where the big
window gave a view of the road. Through her tears she
watched him go. His horse had recovered its health and
carried him jauntily. At the bend Charles turned in the
saddle and sat a moment gazing back at the house. Sally
Day snatched off her big white apron and frantically waved
it, and he saw it and waved, too. Then he rounded the bend
and was gone.

She missed him terribly, and September seemed a long
way off. Now, though, she was caught up in a new excitement. A happy summer began. Her parents approved of
her marriage, and were determined to provide her with the
best trousseau they could afford.

Mrs. Hammond had lavish ideas about trousseaux, for

she had grown up in a wealthy home. Sally Day's father was a man of modest means, dependent on the Emporium for his living. The two never clashed on the subject, though, for Mr. Hammond adored his wife and daughter, and would have gone into debt if his wife had asked him to.

She and Sally Day weren't willing to do that. They decided that the possessions Sally Day took into her married life would be the best they could manage within her father's means.

Now that the war was over and the American ports were open to shipping, beautiful materials were coming in from Europe and the Orient. Mr. Hammond made a trip to New York to buy stock for the store and to choose the materials for Sally Day's trousseau and her supply of linens. When he returned from that trip, with the back of the buggy piled high with bolts of cloth, it was like all Sally Day's Christmases rolled into one.

Only Eugene was unmoved when Mrs. Hammond unwrapped the bolts and draped the lovely materials over the girls. Willie and Sally Day went quite wild with joy, for new gowns had been few and far between during the long years of war. Mr. Hammond beamed, watching his women folk.

He grandly promised Sally Day scores of new dresses, but sober reason prevailed. "Probably the Hornes are simple people like ourselves, and wouldn't welcome a daughter dressed like a peacock," Mrs. Hammond pointed out.

Shortly after that, Miss Trimble arrived. She was the village seamstress, who also sewed for some of the well-to-do families in the great houses of the area. Mr. Hammond had hired her to stay until Sally Day's wardrobe and linens were finished, and she would live with the family.

Perhaps she had expected that for a simple, country girl she would be making only a few calico day dresses and a silk for Sunday. Her eyes almost popped out when she saw the silks, challis, fringes and laces.

She was the fashion arbiter of the locality, so she was the one who decided what Sally Day was to have. She chose two calicos for day dresses, planning to make sunbonnets of the same cottons. A length of Salferino red merino would be stitched into a gown for afternoons. Miss Trimble insisted that Mr. Hammond buy a few yards of black velvet, to make a short basque to go with the merino costume. A dark blue merino would make an elegant traveling dress.

Sally Day eyed a fragile blue silk, imagining an elegant party gown trimmed in fringe perhaps, with a scalloped skirt and a low neck that would leave her arms and shoulders bare. Her own common sense prevailed this time, though. From hints that Charles had let drop she guessed that such a dress would be utterly out of keeping in the life she was going to live, and she reluctantly let it go.

Her mother insisted, however, that she must own a morning dress of cashmere and that of course Miss Trimble must make her the one gown that all married women must own, a plain black for Sunday. For this Mrs. Hammond chose a heavy, ribbed silk. It would last Sally Day for a lifetime and some day would be handed down as an heirloom to her own daughter if she had one.

Her wedding dress was to be of pale, gray silk, light as gossamer. Mr. Hammond had bought the fragile gray slippers that matched it when he purchased the material. Sally Day had a short, sharp battle with Miss Trimble on the subject of hoopskirts. She wanted them but the seamstress said no, that Paris, the world's fashion center, said hoopskirts were out, and that was that. If hoopskirts were out then pantalets were, too, so Sally Day resigned herself to the full skirts and tight bodices of the day. Nevertheless her blue cashmere, her red merino, her black silk and her wedding gown would be richly adorned with fringe, braid, ribbons and beads.

The guest room was converted into a sewing room and there Miss Trimble ruled like a queen. Wilhelmina hung around, endlessly fascinated. She seemed to think her older sister was the most "romantical" girl in the world. She reported to Sally Day, "I heard Miss Trimble tell Mama that sewing for you is like dressing a doll, you're so pretty and small."

The seamstress allowed Willie to stay inside the sewing room as long as she sewed careful stitches, hemming Sally Days' linen petticoats. Willie was Miss Trimble's willing slave, especially when Molly and Sally Day's other friends came to work. Then she sat quietly, listening to the older girls' gossip.

Miss Trimble kept an eagle eye on them all, enforcing her rule that each stitch for hems was to be two threads under, two threads over. She was pleased that Sally Day was so neat and handy with a needle. When Molly and the others complained they would ruin their eyesight sewing so fine, Miss Trimble said it was high time they learned the proper rules.

Lacey White never came, and Molly explained, "That branch of the family's fit to be tied that you're marrying a Yankee, Sally Day."

Sally Day had waited and waited for her cousin to come. She was looking for an excuse anyway to get away from her day-long sewing chores. So she told her mother, "I'm going to pay a call on Aunt Belle and Lacey White and see what ails them."

"Yes, do that," Mrs. Hammond agreed. "We don't want ill feelings with those of your father's folks that favored the South. I suppose they think we're likely to crow over them, or else blame them for the President's death. Take your Aunt Belle a nice glass of jelly and let them know we're just as good kinfolks as we always used to be."

Sally Day didn't get to make the call after all, however. Her father was working hard at the Emporium, and Mrs. Hammond suggested that Sally help him for a few days. "It'll give the child's eyes a rest from her sewing," she suggested.

It was a relief to escape from the stuffy little sewing room. Sally Day dressed up in her best calico and happily rode to town in the buggy. Once there, though, she discovered she wasn't going to take it easy, and hold court because she was engaged to be married. The Emporium was in a thorough mess, the stock mixed up, dust over everything. "You're a mighty poor housekeeper, Papa," she scolded, tying an enormous apron around her waist.

She was rearranging cards of buttons in a case behind the counter when two large hands covered her eyes. "Guess who," a young, male voice said.

"I don't have to guess," she said, tugging at the hands. Tillman picked her up and kissed her.

"Put me down," she ordered.

She realized then that Lacey White and Aunt Belle were watching. "Yes, put her down, for she's practically a married woman now," Lacey White said severely.

Tillman grinned cheerfully. He was looking healthy, and also elegant in a black suit with a ruffled white shirt, far different than he had when Sally Day last saw him in faded Confederate gray. "That's nonsense," he said lightly. "Our dear little cousin isn't going to marry any Yankee."

Sally Day came around the counter and went straight to her Aunt Belle and took her hand. "I'm not going to let any Yankee come between me and my own kin," she said, "so please, Auntie, don't be angry with me."

Her aunt's face softened. "It's true, then?"

"Yes, it's true, I'll marry Mr. Charles Horne in the fall. Lacey White, the girls come every afternoon to help with my sewing. Won't you join us?"

Her cousin hesitated, then agreed. "Yes, I'll come. Don't worry, Sally Day, I've heard all about the lovely things Miss Trimble is making at your house."

Tillman said, "So my own sister is going over to the enemy." His lips smiled, but his eyes didn't. "You know this is nonsense, Sally Day. You can't marry the Yankee because you're going to marry me."

"No, I'm not, and in any case this isn't the place to discuss it," she said tartly.

Soon after that Aunt Bell and Lacey White paid a formal call at the Hammond house, bringing a solid-silver fruit bowl. Sally Day proudly added it to her growing collection of wedding gifts on display in the parlor.

Tillman didn't come to her home, but he haunted the store. He whispered with Sally Day behind the counter, teasing her that the gowns and gifts were being collected for her marriage to him. She became troubled, then annoyed by his attentions. Finally her father noticed what was going on and asked her, "Do you want me to speak to Tillman and put a stop to this?"

"No, Papa," she said, "I guess I can take care of a little old cousin. He's only fooling."

One afternoon when Tillman started his nonsense, she told him, "I'm going home, cousin, and you can drive me."

He practically fell all over himself, gallantly assisting her into his carriage. "Do I have to take you straight home?" he asked.

"No. Let's have a little drive down to the Bay."

"Good! Everyone will see us and know you're my girl."

She didn't answer. She waited until they were well out of town, then took the reins from him and drew the horse to a halt. Surprised, Tillman watched her. She turned back the collar of her dress, and he saw that the gold brooch he had bought in Richmond was fastened there. She said fervently, "I always wear it, Tillman, night and day. It's just a lie I ever agreed to marry Charles Horne, for ever since you gave me the pin I've intended to be your wife. I only wanted you to declare yourself. I just adore you and I know you love me, and now I've got my trousseau practically ready and we can be married any day you say."

His mouth fell open, then he closed it with a snap. "Do you mean it?"

"Of course I do. Oh, maybe it was kind of mean to trick you and trap you, and snatch you away from all the pretty girls in Baltimore. Don't worry, I've heard how you go mooning around after them when you visit there. Even so, you're mine, you've said so yourself. So now we'll tell Papa it's you I'm marrying, and I'll write to poor old Charles Horne and tell him it was just a joke. Giddap!" she called to the horse.

They were halfway back to town before Tillman really got his breath back. Then he took the reins from her and slowed his horse. He demanded suspiciously, "Sally Day, you really mean it."

"Of course I do. I don't give my promise lightly."

"You did to that Yankee."

"I explained. That was only to make you declare your-self."

"Sally Day, I wasn't planning to get married quite yet. Haven't you heard that I'm going to college this fall? My mother wants me to study law. Some day I'll marry you, it's not that I don't want to, please, dear, understand that!"

For answer she unfastened the gold pin and pushed it into his hand. She was surprised herself at how easily her tears started flowing. "You're jilting me!" she sobbed.

He stared at her, aghast. Then he let out a roar of laugh-ter. "You never meant it," he said. "You called my bluff."

"I did, too, mean it!"

"No, you didn't. You're going to marry that black-hearted Yankee. Keep the pin. You've got to, I bought it for you."

"Is it a cousinly gift? You're sure it's not a loverly gift?"

"No, it's for the cutest, wickedest cousin any man ever had. Of course I might want to borrow it back some time, to loan it to one of those Baltimore girls."

Sally Day pinned it at the top of her bodice where it showed. "The Baltimore girls will have to fight me to get hold of it," she said.

When they drove back through town everybody on the street stared, for they were laughing loudly. Tillman was no problem for the rest of the summer.

There were a few small family parties, and her cousin squired her to them. Her dresses, bonnets and hats were finished. Her wedding gifts were packed in crates. The hundred silver dollars her father gave her were tucked into a new leather purse. Her new trunk arrived and stood in her room, waiting to be filled with her trousseau for her journey to Connecticut.

Charles Horne wrote letters which seemed stiff and formal, but in each he spoke of coming to claim her as his wife. At the end of August he set the day. He planned to arrive on September 10.

The first of September came and Sally Day's long summer of waiting was almost over. Now her parents seemed silent and troubled. "Daughter, you're sure you want to marry him?" Mr. Hammond asked.

"Yes, Papa, certain sure," she told him.

"You have no doubts at all?"

"No, Papa, only a few little ones, and they'll go away when he gets here."

It was a very emotional time. Her family was so dear to her, she dreaded leaving them. She took long walks along the canal just to be with the dogs, and Boots and Saddles watched her anxiously, aware there was something different in the air. Gene didn't try to wriggle away when she seized him and hugged him and Willie tagged after her.

She caught her mother sprinkling her brand new handkerchiefs with tears instead of cologne, and they had a good weep together. "Oh, Mama, Connecticut isn't so far away that I can't get home to see you," Sally Day whispered.

"It can be a very long way, once you're married," her mother warned. "Then you'll belong to your husband and his people, and that's right, that's the way it ought to be. So don't mind if I shed a few tears, darling. Mothers always cry."

Those last few days, when everything was ready and she had only to wait for Charles, Sally Day moved quietly around the house. She was memorizing it, getting the view of the back garden and the canal by heart so she'd have them to take to Connecticut with her. She kept her family in view, wanting to look at them so she could take them, too.

The cooking was done for the wedding lunch. Exhausted by the final day of baking, Sally Day and her mother were resting on the bench in the orchard at dusk, watching the children and the hounds coming up from the canal, waiting for Mr. Hammond to arrive home for supper. A clop, clop of horse's hooves rang in the road and stopped at the gate. Sally Day's heart thudded painfully. Her husband had arrived.

Chapter Seven

THE NEXT MORNING when Sally Day awakened her mother was leaning over her. "Happy is the bride the sun shines on," Mrs. Hammond said. It was true; glorious sunshine illuminated the September day. Sally Day buttoned on an old calico gown and hurried downstairs to help, for a great deal of work still had to be done.

After breakfast Charles hung around, looking miserable, knowing he was in the way. Sally Day was seeing him for the first time in civilian clothes, and kept glancing at him. In his black broadcloth suit, with a snowy white shirt, he looked thin and distinguished in a romantic way. He was pale, though. Was he as scared as she was, Sally Day wondered.

Her father finally took pity on the bridegroom and carried him off to the Emporium, to get him out of the world of women.

For a simple wedding of only fifty guests, the work seemed endless. Some of the cousins arrived to help, and Mrs. Hammond was sent upstairs to dress the bride.

Eugene had made endless trips to carry water up to Sally Day's room, so she could bathe in the tub. Clean, with her shining dark hair tumbling below her waist, she called her mother to help her.

Her waist was so small she didn't need much pulling to make her corset tight, but she was jumping around so, her mother said, "Stand still, Sally Day, this is like trying to lace up a grasshopper!"

Sally Day's teeth chattered. "Oh, Mama, I'm scared out of my wits!"

"Every woman's scared, just before," her mother said comfortingly.

"Is that true?"

"Yes. I remember that I wanted to run off where your father would never find me. Yet I knew I'd swim oceans to get to him. Do you feel that way, too, child? Because it's not too late to change your mind, if your fears are real."

Sally Day said, relieved, "I'm scared to marry him, but I'm scareder not to."

Her mother slipped the gray silk gown over her head and helped button it and adjusted the sash. Sally Day put on her white cotton stockings, then her silk wedding slippers. Mrs. Hammond brushed the long hair and drew it tightly back in a heavy chignon. At last she stood back and gazed at her daughter. "It's wrong to flatter you," she whispered, "but I've got to tell you, you are utterly beautiful."

They knew that Wilhelmina was hovering just outside the door. Now she called, "I'm her sister so I ought to see her first. I've got a right."

"Yes, sister, come in, you've got a right," Sally Day called back. They hugged carefully, not to muss each other. Willie was looking very pretty in a new red delaine that set off her ashen hair. The two girls waited while their mother dressed in her best Sunday silk. From below came laughter and chatter as the guests arrived.

Charles was with her father in the kitchen, Sally Day knew. Finally Mr. Hammond called up the back stairs, "Everybody's here. It's time, girls."

Sally Day smoothed her long kid gloves, grasped her silk-covered Bible. She paused at the top of the stairs, looking down into a sea of friendly faces. Her eyes found Charles standing beside the minister and her father at the other side of the room, and she noted with satisfaction that Charles was really overcome at the first sight of her in her wedding gown. Gene was waiting on the stairs, and had the same awed look, and she quietly leaned down to hug him. Then the crowd parted and she stood beside the man she had chosen.

She tried to listen to the words that the minister said over them, but she caught only a few phrases. Charles's voice rang out loudly in his responses, and Sally Day spoke up clearly, to let the whole world know she loved this man. Very soon it was over and they were man and wife. Charles leaned down to kiss her reverently, and someone in the party called, "Pick her up, Mr. Horne, for she's no bigger than a minute!"

Everyone laughed and crowded around to kiss the bride. Tillman's strong arms gathered her in, and over his shoulder Sally Day caught a glimpse of her husband's frowning face. In that moment she realized that the war hadn't been over long enough for these two to lose their bitterness toward each other. She grasped Charles's hand and made him take Tillman's. "You two must like each other, because I love you both," she said.

They eyed each other sternly. Then Tillman said, "Hello, Yank," and Charles's thin mouth curved in a smile as he said, "How are you, Reb?"

Some of the cousins and aunts were serving the wedding lunch in the dining room. It seemed queer to Sally Day to be a guest, not helping her mother see that all were served, their plates piled high with turkey and ham and salad, shortbread and preserves. She moved among the guests, clutching her husband's hand. It was lovely to hear them welcoming him into the family.

Aunt Belle didn't exactly welcome him, though. She fixed him with her eagle eye and said gruffly, "It's too bad your mother and father didn't come to see you married."

The Hammonds had felt badly, too, that Mr. and Mrs. Horne had not come in answer to Sally Day's written invitation. Charles said now, "They don't leave the farm."

That seemed like a queer remark. Aunt Belle said, "Do you mean they never go visiting?" She seemed to find this hard to believe, because Maryland people were always traveling around to each other's houses to stay for weeks at a time.

Tillman had a mischievous look in his blue eyes, when he joined the group. He said heartily, "You know, Mr. Horne, you're a lucky man to be carrying off my cousin, for she's one of the prettiest girls in Maryland. You'll need your luck, too, for she'll lead you a dance, you can be sure of that."

Charles's answer made Sally Day smile up at her tall cousin in triumph, for her husband said drily, "I thank you for your good advice, Mr. Wyatt, but I expect I'll manage."

The day was wearing on. Finally Mrs. Hammond and Molly and some of the other cousins spirited Sally Day upstairs to dress for traveling. They helped her into the dark-blue merino. She perched a tiny, blue velvet hat on top of her head, and exchanged her slippers for her high gaiters. There were "ohs" and "ahs" to meet her when she came down again.

She almost went to pieces when it came time to kiss her parents and Willie and Gene goodbye, and frantically longed to change her mind, to stay within the comfortable safety of home. Her husband's grasp was firm on her elbow though when Mr. Hammond handed her over to him, saying, "Take good care of our little girl, Charles." Everyone rushed to kiss her, and Charles whisked her though the crowd and lifted her into a rented carriage.

She knelt on the seat waving goodbye, crying and laughing until her dear, familiar home was out of sight. Charles understood and gave her his handkerchief to cry into and patted her shoulder clumsily.

They reached Elkton at midafternoon, and the train was in the station to carry them through the dusk to New York. Sally Day recovered from her grief at leaving home, and sparkled and laughed during the drive in a hansom cab to the hotel where they were to spend their first night. The city impressed her, and the splendor of the hotel awed her. Actually though, she chattered because she was nervous at the thought of being alone with a strange, new husband.

When her relatives first learned she was engaged to marry a Yankee, one of her aunts had asked, "Sally Day, are you positive this Mr. Horne is a gentleman?"

"I don't reckon I know for sure what a gentleman is," Sally Day had answered, nettled by the implied criticism.

She realized the following morning, when she sat across from Charles in the elegant dining room at breakfast, she was still not sure what a gentleman was, but she knew one thing: she had married a gentle man. When she gazed at him across the table, such love welled up in her heart that her eyes filled with tears.

He grew silent, though, on the long train ride through the green Connecticut countryside. She took his hand and played with his fingers, and finally asked him, "Cat got your tongue?"

He bent his dark look on her. She came just to his shoulder, sitting close to him. He said, "Sally Day, I don't feel easy in my mind. I've tried to tell you that your ways aren't always our ways, in Jericho, though for the life of me I can't tell which are best. My parents will love you when they come to know you, but they may seem strange, and you may seem strange to them. Will you give them a chance to get used to you?"

She gazed up at him, surprised. "Why, Charles, I'll love them on sight, I know I will! And what's strange about me?"

"I can't explain," he said helplessly.

They said no more. The train drew into a small station and Charles said, "We're here."

"But where's the town? Where's Jericho?" she asked, after they had climbed down to the platform and Sally Day's boxes and trunks had been taken off, and the train chugged away.

"The town's just down the road," Charles explained.

A horse harnessed to a farm wagon was nodding at the rail. The station agent emerged, and sauntered over. "Hello, Charlie. Would it help you any if I drove you out to your place?"

"It sure would, Eph," Charles replied.

He lifted Sally Day by her elbows up to the high seat, and the men piled her belongings in the back. "I take it this is your bride I heard tell of," Eph said. "She sure comes heavy loaded!"

He picked up the reins and called, "Giddap." Sally Day turned to him, determined to make friends with this first acquaintance. "You haven't seen anything," she said brightly. "My folks will be shipping my wedding gifts and then maybe you'll be so kind as to tote them out for us, too."

She sat between the two men, trying to see everything she could of Jericho, exclaiming how pretty the little town looked with its white houses, neat yards, tall elms arching over the main street. She chattered with Eph and thought, If all Jericho folks are as friendly as he is, I'll have no trouble at all. He chuckled at her sallies and said he had never realized Charlie Horne had such a knowing eye for a pretty gal.

"Here you are, Mrs. Horne," he said finally, pulling up at the end of a rocky lane before a farmhouse under towering trees. Dark had come down, but there wasn't a light in the house.

"Are you sure this is the place?" Sally Day asked nervously. Then she laughed, "I guess my husband ought to know his own home."

"They'd be in the kitchen this time of evening," Charles explained.

Eph helped him set her trunks and boxes beside the road. Sally Day shivered, suddenly chilled, exhausted by the long day. A light in the doorway and someone calling "Welcome," would have made all the difference in this arrival. But the house loomed dark and silent.

"Be seeing you, Mrs. Horne," Eph called, and clattered off.

Charles took Sally Day's elbow to guide her as they circled the house in the pitch dark. Somewhere a dog was barking furiously. Charles stopped once, said hoarsely, "Just try to do what's right, Sally Day, and it will all work out."

A light glimmered through the windows in back. Sally Day caught a glimpse of two people seated at the kitchen table. The man stood up, hearing their footsteps. He looked immensely tall, tall enough to touch the ceiling. They waited on the stone step while he unbolted the door. This seemed very strange to Sally Day, coming from a place where nobody ever locked a door.

It swung open. Mr. Horne picked up the lamp to show them in. Sally Day paused outside, not knowing whether to laugh or to cry. Nobody rushed to kiss her, nobody even said, "How are you?" much less, "Welcome."

"Come in, don't stand there," Mrs. Horne called. "You're letting in the mosquitoes."

Sally Day moved across the threshold. Charles didn't pick her up and carry her over it as he should have done. But he was close beside her and she grasped his arm. "How do you do?" she said, and added idiotically, "I'm Sally Day Hammond."

"You're Mrs. Horne," her father-in-law stated. "That's what we understood Charles went to Maryland for, to marry himself a wife."

Chapter Eight

JUST TWO MORNINGS AGO, Sally Day realized, she had awakened to her mother's kiss and remark, "Happy the bride the sun shines on." Well, on this first morning in her new home the sun was still shining, but it seemed to Sally Day it was a thinner sun, and cooler.

Now it was eight o'clock, and she felt as though she had been up for a whole day. The night before she and Charles had gone up to their room soon after they arrived, for Sally Day was very tired. She had only the dimmest memory of sitting at the kitchen table and eating a bowl of soup, then of being led upstairs by the light of her mother-in-law's candle. She had seen that the room was vast and empty and clean, before she tumbled into the big fourposter. She sank into the feather bed and slept immediately.

Her husband had awakened her, "Sally Day, it's time to get up."

The candle made only a small pool of light, and the windows were pitch black. "It's the middle of the night," she had protested.

"No, dawn will soon break."

"But that's only five o'clock! Who gets up at five o'clock?"

"Everyone does."

She had tried to argue, "I never got up at such an hour in my whole life."

He was gentle but firm. "Sally Day, we want to make the right start. On a farm the clock is different. Be a good girl and get dressed and come down as soon as you can. I'll be out in the barn helping Pa with the milking."

Charles had said only one thing that made sense, that Sally Day wanted to make the right start. She quickly dressed by the flickering candle, parted and piled her hair on top of her head, whisked a light powdering of cornmeal over her face, and trotted down the back stairs.

Mrs. Horne was bent over, taking something out of the oven of the great iron range, when Sally Day caroled, "Good morning!" She straightened up. "Goodness, child, you gave me a fright!"

All her life Sally Day had known that when she smiled at the world, the world smiled back at her. This worked now, and her mother-in-law's stern face softened. "What can I do to help?" Sally Day asked.

"You can set the table if you've a mind to. You'll find the dishes on the Dutch cupboard over there."

Sally Day took off the red-checked table cover and shook it out the door. She saw that the gray light of morning was glowing in the east. A lantern flickered in the huge barn fifty yards away.

She took down the stone-china plates and carefully placed them, found cups and spoons and forks. "Where are the napkins, Mother?" she asked.

Mrs. Horne stiffened. Was it the word "Mother" that startled her? Sally Day wondered what she ought to call Charles's mother, but hadn't gotten around to asking him. Mrs. Horne said, "We don't use napkins for breakfast,

Sarah."

"I reckon we've got to decide what I'm going to be called," Sally Day said cheerfully. "Sarah is my mother's name. Mine is Sally Day."

"You mean that's actually your rightful name?"

"That's how it's written in the records."

"Two names together like that? Is that how southern people do?"

"It's how many of them do. My cousin, now, she's Lacey White. It's easier to keep us straight, by adding some family name, if there are a lot of Sallys and Laceys in a family."

Mrs. Horne didn't answer, and Sally Day said, "Do you mind very much?"

"No, it doesn't bother me too much," Mrs. Horne said reluctantly, "but it may take some time for Mr. Horne and me to feel easy saying it."

This matter of names was getting more complicated by the minute. Sally Day decided to let pass this surprising fact that his own wife called Ezra Horne "Mister." "I'm afraid I'll have trouble answering to Sarah," she said lightly.

"The other might sound somewhat heathenish in his ears."

"Heathenish!"

"They're coming," the older woman warned.

The men stamped the mud off their feet before they entered, then washed at the sink and took their places. Sally Day chirped, "Good morning," but it fell on deaf ears.

For the first time she was seeing her husband in work clothes. She went to him and leaned on his shoulder, needing reassurance. He smelled of the barn, of animal sweat and manure, and her nose wrinkled. Nevertheless she bent closer, wanting his arm around her. He patted her hand

and ordered, "Take your place, Sally Day."

Breakfast was eaten in silence. Sally Day only toyed with hers, because the food was so heavy. At home she would have taken a cup of coffee and a piece of toast. Now she was faced with fried potatoes, eggs, sausage, oatmeal and apple pie. Mrs. Horne noticed and said kindly, "You're not used to our food or our ways yet, Sarah. Is there anything special you'd like?"

Mr. Horne glanced up from under his gray, heavy brows and said, "Sarah will have to take us as she finds us." Silence greeted this and he added, "Speak up, girl, it doesn't do any harm to speak up."

Sally Day said nervously, "I always think a cup of coffee or tea is easier to start the day on. I can make it myself."

"We don't have coffee and tea's for when the minister comes to call," Mr. Horne stated.

"Then I reckon I'll just have to wait until the minister comes to get my tea," Sally Day said with a laugh.

Mrs. Horne sat rigid and Mr. Horne's eyes widened and he looked at Sally Day as though he was really seeing her for the first time. Charles flashed her a look she couldn't exactly interpret, except that it wasn't angry. His father growled, "If you must have tea, then go and get it, girl."

She could have backed down and said, "I really don't care," or "I don't want to be extra trouble." Instead she marched over to the stove and set the kettle over the hottest plate. When she came back to the table with her tea steaming in a thick cup, Mr. Horne paid no attention to it or her. He was outlining for Charles the day's work that lay before them.

The men got up and went out. Sally Day cleared the table. Her mother-in-law didn't speak, but Sally Day was beginning to think that silence didn't always mean disapproval. These people just weren't in the habit of talking. It was utterly unlike home, where the house was so full of chatter all day long that her own father sometimes complained he lived in a nest of sparrows.

The water pails were empty and she picked them up to go to the well in the barnyard. Mrs. Horne said, "Put them down, Sarah. You're only a slip of a thing and couldn't lift them."

"Maybe I'm not very big, but I'm strong," Sally Day said earnestly. "I've never had a sick day in my life."

However, Mrs. Horne was right, the pails were so heavy Sally Day staggered under their weight. She managed to carry them in, however, and set them on the drainboard. She went to her room, then, to hang up her dresses.

They had gotten sadly mussed in the trunk. She took the time to smooth each one lovingly before she hung it on the hooks that lined one wall. She laid out the red merino to wear for dinner.

She found she was tip-toeing when she came down the broad, uncarpeted front stairs. Chickens clucked in the yard, but there wasn't a sound in the house. She found her mother-in-law in the downstairs bedroom, off the kitchen. Mrs. Horne was carding wool, energetically yanking the carder through the tangled skein, and lint flew. She said, "Maybe you'd like to finish this for me, while I start the dinner."

Quite willingly Sally Day took the carder and tried to imitate the older woman's deft strokes, but soon the skein was more tangled than before. She said, "I reckon maybe my mother neglected my education, but I'll learn. I learn pretty fast."

"Who did the carding in your house?"

"Nobody. My father owns the general store in Chesapeake City, so we get our cloth ready made."

"Here nothing's ready made," Mrs. Horne said. "We do it all ourselves."

"Maybe you'd show me how, this afternoon. I want to be useful, oh, I really want to very much!"

Again she set the table, and this time Mrs. Horne allowed her to help with the cooking, whipping the potatoes and serving the applesauce and cutting the pie. When everything was ready and they were waiting for the men, Sally Day ran upstairs and quickly slipped into the red merino. She was still buttoning the bodice when she came down, for she was afraid of delaying dinner.

She needn't have worried, they had started without her. Three surprised faces turned in her direction. Mrs. Horne spoke for them all. "Why did you put on your best dress? You're not going anywhere."

Now what had she done wrong? At home she and her mother and Willie always put on an afternoon dress for the noonday meal. "I thought everybody changed for dinner," she stammered.

"Calico or linsey-woolsey does for all day here," Mrs. Horne said.

Sally Day almost said what was on the tip of her tongue, that in Maryland only poor white trash wore the cheap weave of linen and wool called linsey-woolsey. She was confused and she was beginning to get angry, because everything she did or said put her in a worse light, and it was not her fault, no it was not.

Charles rescued her. He didn't jump up to help her with her chair as a man would have done at home, but he smiled at her. He said, "She needs a warmer dress because there's a chill in the air and I've promised to take her around to see the farm this afternoon. There's something in the barn she ought to see."

Sally Day gave him a grateful look. He hadn't promised any such thing, he was helping her to get away from the house.

"That gate's got to be mended," Mr. Horne warned him.

"The gate will get mended before dark, Pa."

The disapproval in the air was so real Sally Day felt she could brush it away like a cobweb, and her heart was heavy. The last thing in the world she wanted was to cause dissension between Charles and his parents, but she seemed to be doing exactly that.

Just the same she was so relieved to escape from the house into the bright, September sunshine, her heart turned light again. Charles led her to the barn. Chickens scooted out of the way, and she stepped carefully to protect her new black gaiters.

The barn seemed empty, for the cows were out to pasture, but in one corner, in a dimly lit stall, Sally Day saw what Charles had brought her out for. A cow stood in the straw, her newly born calf butting her side. "Oh, the pretty thing," Sally Day whispered. The fragile black-and-white calf wobbled over on pipe-stem legs and thrust its narrow head between the boards. Sally Day put out her hand and it nuzzled her fingers with its clean, soft lips. "How old is it?" she asked.

"It was born before daybreak. I thought you'd like it."

"Charles, how wonderful! This beautiful thing happened on my very first morning."

"It's not a great occasion to have a new calf born on a

farm."

"It is to me. I never saw such a young one before."

He took her hand and they went out. A dog that had been sleeping in the sun got to its feet and came over, but its tail didn't wag. Did the dog expect that she was going to hit him? Sally Day put out her hand palm up, and the dog sniffed. Then his tail began to move, and he turned deep brown eyes up to her. "What's his name?" she asked.

"He doesn't have one," Charles said. "He's just the dog who brings in the cows."

"Whoever heard of a dog without a name? I'll give him one," she said gaily.

She took Charles's hand and swung it as they walked on. He glanced back nervously, and she guessed he was thinking his parents might be watching, but she didn't let go of his hand. Beyond the barn they descended a little hill, where a brook meandered through a meadow. They crossed on stepping stones and came to woods. "Are we still on your father's land?" Sally Day asked.

"Oh, yes. Pa's got four hundred acres now."

"I don't know how much that is, but it sounds like a lot. Then your father is rich?"

"No, it's fair land, but he has to scratch to get a living off it. Come, I'll show you the two-hundred-acre piece he deeded over to me for our marriage gift. He gave us a third of his holding."

"You said he might do that but I didn't know he already had," Sally Day said. "Charles, I reckon I don't understand. Ever since I got here he's acted as though he disliked the idea of your marrying me. But that was a mighty generous gift."

"Give him time," Charles said, troubled. "It takes

Connecticut people a long time to get used to newcomers and their ways."

They emerged from the wood and climbed over a stone wall, entering a cleared field that bordered the road. "This is ours," Charles said. "It runs three hundred yards along the road to the row of maples, then corners back to that tallest pine you can see, way up there. It's prime land, my father didn't niggle over that."

"It's the most beautiful land in the world! Does it have a piece of brook?"

"Yes, it's got a nice piece of brook," he said, smiling down at her.

Sally Day sank down, pulling him with her. "The ground's damp and you'll catch your death of cold," he warned.

"Oh, bother that! Look, Charles, down here we own as far as we can see! We own the whole world."

For answer he gathered her in his arms and gave her a long, long kiss. She closed her eyes, feeling his careful hand smoothing back her hair. "Oh, Charles, I'm so terribly happy that you brought me here," she whispered.

"Do you mean it?"

"Yes, I mean it."

The dog had come up and was watching curiously. She put out her hand, and the shaggy beast came closer and licked it. "I'll feel even happier when I think of the right name for you, dog," she said contentedly.

Charles reminded her again she was catching her death of dampness, and they got up and started home. "I've heard that when October comes and the trees turn, New England gets so beautiful a body can hardly bear it," Sally Day said. "I'm glad I'm going to see that."

"You're not sorry you came?" Charles asked. "Sally Day,

do you truly think you'll be happy here?"

"Why, you great big ninny," she cried, "I'm the happiest girl in the world right now!"

Chapter Nine

SALLY DAY WAS composing her first letter home. "Dear Mother, I hope this finds you in good health, as it leaves me. We arrived safely on the train to New York and stayed at an elegant hotel."

She wrote carefully, for she felt like a world traveler now, having come so far from home, and wanted to give exactly the right tone. "Our room looked down on Fifth Avenue, and I'm sure that neither Paris nor London could offer a more cosmopolitan view."

Having left New York behind, she relaxed into a more conversational tone. "We came to Connecticut the next afternoon, and the station master at Jericho drove us to the Hornes' house. He's a funny, friendly man and I hope to see him again. He was the very first person to call me by my married title.

"Now I will tell you all about Connecticut and the Hornes' house. This country is quite beautiful, with big farms. The Hornes have six hundred acres, or rather, four hundred. They gave Charles and me two hundred for our marriage present; wasn't that a lovely thing to do? We don't know when we'll build our own dear little house on our own land, so for awhile we'll go on living with Charles's parents. Their house has twelve rooms, I hear, but I haven't seen them all because some are shut up. We have a large bedroom. It is cold but has a wonderful feather mattress."

Now she had come to the hard part, describing her mother- and father-in-law. Sally Day bit her quill pen with her white teeth, thinking hard. This letter would be passed around her aunts and cousins to be read, for nobody in the Hammond or Wyatt or Gans families had ever moved North. Anything she said would be of interest. If only she was sitting with her mother on the bench under the apple tree, watching the barges passing along the canal, then she could unburden her heart. Now she must be careful what she said, for she didn't want any suspicions that all was not well with her to circulate among her relatives.

The thought of her wise, cheerful mother and how she longed to see her caused Sally Day a spasm of homesickness. She got up and walked around the bedroom, for the longing was a physical pain that caught her unawares. She hadn't expected anything like this. It was several moments before she mastered the feeling and went back to her letter.

"Mr. and Mrs. Horne are quiet people. That is why Charles doesn't talk much, I think. They work hard, for this is a big farm, and soon I'll learn their ways and then I'll be able to help. I didn't know, for instance, that people card their own wool and weave their own cloth. Papa spoiled us, didn't he, bringing such lovely materials home from the store?

"There are forty head of cattle on the farm. You don't count tails or feet, you count heads. There is a flock of sheep which seem rather stupid, but perhaps they aren't. There is a clever shepherd dog who brings the cows in from the fields, who wants to be my friend. The Hornes will let me name him. I haven't any idea how many Rhode Island red chickens there are. They run to me squawking when I shake out the crumbs from the table.

"Mr. Horne calls me 'Sarah.' I haven't been able to explain to him yet that I'm truly named 'Sally Day.' In many things our Maryland ways are not the ways of people here, but that is not to say that ours are better or worse.

"They don't have parties here as we do at home, but I daresay when the word gets around there is a new bride in the neighborhood there will be one or two.

"Mr. Horne's barn is very big and almost as fine as his house.

"There, Mama, I have told you a few things about my new life. The next time when I know more about it I will write a longer letter. I forgot to say that ladies wear linsey-woolsey here and it is not a disgrace. And there is something else I thought of. Molly told me that her cousin in Delaware would be married soon and asked if she might borrow my wedding dress. I said no but now I think that was selfish, and besides I will have fewer opportunities to wear gray silk than I expected. So will you tell Molly to tell her cousin she may borrow my gown and I will send it and she is welcome to wear it. Your loving daughter, Sally Day Horne, Sally Day Hammond that was."

She hastily addressed the letter. Charles would mail it from town the next time he went to the store. She wanted to get away from her room and run outdoors, for maybe out there she would escape from the sudden homesickness that made her want to bury her head in the feather bed and weep.

Just then Mrs. Horne passed along the hall. She glanced in, and must have seen in Sally Day's face something of what she was feeling, for she hesitated. "Sarah, are you well?"

"Oh, yes, I'm quite well. I've just been writing to my mother. Please come in."

Mrs. Horne looked around. "You have a great many dresses, child."

Sally Day was delighted that she noticed and took an interest. "My parents didn't want you to be ashamed that Charles chose me for your daughter-in-law," she said brightly.

Mrs. Horne said slowly, "The number and splendor of a girl's dresses are not important. Her character is."

Sally Day laughed. "When you get better acquainted with me, Mother, you'll know I have a splendid character!"

"Fine feathers don't make fine birds."

"No, but they help."

Mrs. Horne looked really upset then. "Sarah, that is a light and wayward thing to say."

"I know, it just slipped out," Sally Day apologized. "Anyway, Charles knew when he married me that I love pretty clothes. Didn't you used to when you were a young girl?"

Mrs. Horne rubbed the black silk of Sally Day's Sunday gown between her fingers, then felt the light gray silk of the wedding gown. "I never in my whole life owned any so fine," she murmured.

"I'm sorry," Sally Day said softly. "I don't want you to think I was bragging or that my father is rich. He isn't at all. I couldn't have nice things if he didn't buy them wholesale for the store."

"I came up to speak to you about your appearance," Mrs. Horne said abruptly. "There's no need for you to bother to dress up in the afternoon. Calico does for a farm woman all day. That's the custom here. Folks hereabouts might think a woman was light-minded if she wore lace and fringe and such in daytime."

Trying to understand, Sally Day said uncertainly, "Are you requesting, Mother?"

"Yes, I'm requesting, Sarah. And that's another thing, what you call me. I think probably, because you're only sixteen, and we're not blood relations, Mrs. Horne would be better, for awhile anyway."

So hurt she couldn't even assess how hurt she actually was, Sally Day said quietly, "Yes, Mrs. Horne."

Her voice must have shown it, though. The older woman said hastily, "It'll just be a matter of time, Sarah. Soon it'll come natural for us to call each other differently. I daresay I'll learn to call you Sally Day, though it does sound hea-thenish to my ears right now.

"You're a good child, I'm sure of that. And perhaps on the farm here we live in a backwater and don't know the easier ways of the world. Have patience with us, Sarah, and we'll have patience with you, and everything will work out in the end."

She wanted to take a step toward being friends, Sally Day knew it. But her own hurt and her bleak loneliness were all Sally Day could manage right at that moment. She said coldly, "Yes, Mrs. Horne."

She started from the room. Her mother-in-law put out a hand to stop her but she brushed by.

She didn't want to see anybody, even her husband, just then. She ran through the yard, past the barn, across the meadow and the brook to the woods beyond. She was cry-ing and couldn't see and blundered into trees. She reached a clearing, where moss and princess pine made a soft car-pet, and sank down and clasped her knees, bending her head, torn with sobs.

A cold nose touched her hand. The cow dog had followed her, and his eyes looked concerned and worried. She put out her arms and gathered him in. He wasn't used to such treatment, obviously, but he let her hold him. Soon he relaxed and leaned against her, and began to lick her neck with his warm tongue.

She laughed shakily, pulled him around so she could rest her face on his shaggy head. "Do you like me, dog? I'm glad somebody does," she told him. "You're in the same fix I'm in, I reckon. They won't call me by my right name, but they don't care enough about you even to give you one."

She thought for awhile. He was just a common dog that nobody cared about, so what he needed was a name with some dignity. She tried Prince in her mind, then Duke. She settled on Duke. "Here, Duke. Duke, do you like me?"

For answer he moved closer, and his tail, tangled with burdocks, wagged tentatively. Sally Day pushed him down in her lap, took the tortoise shell comb out of her back hair and gave him a thorough combing, starting at his head, ending with his tail. She hurt him and he whimpered when she yanked too hard. But when she finished his brown coat was smooth and even shone.

She had started out this day determined to be meek and mild, to learn to please her in-laws and be the kind of a daughter they wanted. Now as she murmured to the dog, working over him, a new kind of resolution stiffened her. The difference was that she had found a friend. Not everybody on this farm disapproved of her. The way Duke pushed against her showed he appreciated her.

She heard a voice then, calling "Sally, Sally Day." She

wiped her face with her handkerchief, then took the little bag of scented meal from her pocket and wiped it again, to take away the shine of tears. "I'm coming, Charles," she called.

He looked very relieved when he saw her coming toward him through the thin woods. Right away, though, he had to say something to correct her. "Sally Day, you shouldn't be walking in the woods alone."

"I wasn't alone. Duke was with me."

"Isn't that kind of a fancy name for a mongrel dog?" he asked, faintly smiling.

"Is there a law in Connecticut against fancy names? Is that why I have to answer to Sarah instead of to my proper name?" she countered, tartly.

His face darkened with unhappiness. "Sally Day, I've told you it will take time for you and them to get used to each other."

He was her husband and it was her own mother who had told her it was her duty to make him happy. Sally Day took his arm and said, "I'll try to do better, truly I will."

"I came to fetch you because I'm going to town and thought you might like to come along," he said.

Right away Sally Day's spirits soared. She broke away from her husband and picked up her skirts and ran across the field, with Duke running beside her, wildly barking. Mrs. Horne looked up when she burst into the kitchen. "Oh, Mrs. Horne, Charles and I are going to town!" she cried. "Why don't you come with us? You've been working so hard, you need a little rest!"

Her mother-in-law acted stunned at the suggestion. "I can't off to town in the middle of a workday."

"Why not?"

Mrs. Horne didn't give a reason, she only said, "Of course I can't go, but you go along."

Charles was harnessing a horse to the wagon when Sally Day ran out, clutching her shawl around her shoulders. Duke came to meet her and she announced, "We'll take him, too. He deserves a good time." The dog looked as astonished as Mrs. Horne had, for Sally Day seized him by the scruff of his neck and boosted him into the back of the wagon. They set out.

She moved closer to Charles on the high, hard seat, linking her arm in his. He couldn't seem to take his eyes from her face. Finally she asked, "What are you staring at, Charles?"

"I'm thinking I'm the luckiest man who ever lived," he said.

"You're not sorry you married me? Even if I upset your home and do things wrong and stir up trouble?"

He said seriously, "I'm caught plumb in the middle, Sally Day. You come first of course, but I can see their point of view. Also, they're still grieving over my brother's death, and that's one reason they're so silent."

She whispered, "Oh, Charles. I keep forgetting that. They never mention Ben."

"It's not our way to talk of what means most to us," Charles said.

"But you should. If people talk something out, then it doesn't hurt so much."

"Maybe you're right, but it's not our way," Charles repeated. "Besides—" He stopped.

"Besides, what?"

"Nothing."

"Charles, go on, I order you to."

"All right, but try to understand," Charles said. "My parents can't help thinking of you as a Southerner."

"Maryland isn't so southern, it's a border state," Sally Day said. "What's that got to do with anything?"

"The way your people feel about Yankees is the way some folks up here feel about Southerners. The war hasn't been over long enough for them to begin to forget."

"My own father was for the Union," she reminded him.

"I know, I've told them."

Sally Day considered this, then decided to forget the problem. "I think you're making a great big mountain out of a little mole hill," she said. "Now let's have a good time. Oh, dearest, look around! This is really beautiful country. I never would have guessed it would be so green, now that summer's over."

Not far off the top of a maple had turned to flame. Poison ivy was running scarlet along stone walls that edged the road. "Oh, how wonderful," she breathed.

"Wait until all the trees show color," Charles said.

They reached the top of a long hill. Below in the valley lay Jericho, and in the clear sunlight the white houses gleamed among the trees and a tall spire of a white church pierced the sky. A blue, winding river cut the town in two. "I never imagined anything so pretty in my whole life," Sally Day said. "I'm very, very glad that I came to Jericho to live."

Chapter Ten

AFTER SALLY DAY had made one visit to Jericho, she longed for Sunday to roll around so that she could go again. She had never thought of church-going as an especially exciting adventure, but now she looked forward to it eagerly.

To her relief, the day dawned warm and clear. She was planning on wearing her Sunday gown of black silk for the first time, but had worried that she might have to cover it up with her cloak. As soon as breakfast was over and she had helped with the dishes and had fed the chickens and made her bed, she devoted herself to the serious business of dressing for church.

She wished she knew her husband well enough to ask him to help lace her, but she managed alone. Her waist was only fifteen inches, and didn't need tight lacing. She pulled on her long drawers, put on her corset cover and over those her petticoat. Then she added two more starched petticoats, to make her skirt stand out.

She carefully did up her hair, piling it high and anchoring it with her best gold comb. Then came the great moment. She had no mirror except the small one that hung over her bureau. She set that on the floor. Then she put on

the heavy black gown, careful not to muss her hair. She
straightened the narrow, white collar and pinned it with
the gold brooch Tillman had given her. Then at last she
looked, turning the mirror this way and that until she had
seen herself from all views.

The dress was perfect, fitting like a kid glove. Its full
skirt rustled richly.

Last of all Sally Day set her black velvet hat on her hair
and pinned it securely. She folded her new lace mantilla,
carefully draped it around her shoulders, and primly descended the stairs.

The surrey was ready, for Charles had washed it early
that morning. Mr. Horne, looking taller and more gaunt
than ever in his Sunday black, sat holding the reins, his
wife beside him. Charles was waiting to help Sally Day,
and she put her foot on the step and hopped up lightly as a
bird. "Do I look all right for church?" she asked, but she
was serenely sure of the answer.

Neither of the elder Hornes spoke, and Charles's answer
was a quick squeeze of her hand, but he wore the anxious
look that seemed to be his usual expression these days.

He and Sally Day continued to hold hands. Sally Day
caught Mrs. Horne's words, when she leaned over to whis-
per to her husband, "Remember, she's only a child." His
lips tightened in reply.

With Charles holding her hand Sally Day felt quite brave.
"Is there something wrong with my appearance?" she asked.

Mrs. Horne turned and gave her a wintry smile. "We
don't usually wear velvet and silk and lace to church. It
doesn't seem fitting, Sarah."

"My mother had this dress made especially so I'd be proper
for church. I don't know as it's going to bother the Lord

very much if it's silk and not wool," Sally Day said gaily.

Mrs. Horne swung around to face the road. Her husband's mouth tightened even more.

Sally Day forgot their disapproval though when Charles tied the horse to the bar and they joined the people moving toward the church's wide door. "Well, if it isn't the new little Mrs. Horne!" a hearty voice called.

Sally Day had met Mr. Strong, the proprietor of Jericho's general store, on her first trip to town. Now he gallantly tipped his hat and introduced his wife. This lady had such a cheery, open face, Sally Day warmed to her. "I declare, your husband made me feel right at home, when my Charles took me in his store the other day," she confided. "My own father runs just such a store in Maryland, and I've helped him tend it."

Charles finally had to pull her away. His parents were waiting at the top of the church steps.

Mr. Horne was an elder, and didn't sit with his family during the first part of the service. The Hornes' pew was halfway down the aisle, and Sally Day twisted around to watch the congregation gathering. They seemed like a pleasant lot of people, and the girls and younger women stared and smiled at Sally Day, so naturally she smiled back. The minister, too, was young, and his voice was strong and resonant. Sally Day quite enjoyed the singing and Bible reading.

When the time came for the collection, her father-in-law marched down the middle aisle to pass the collection box on its long stick. Sally Day then had a chance to compare him with the other men. He was handsome, but his stern, stony face set him apart. The collection over, he came forward and took the aisle seat in the Hornes' pew, next to his wife.

There was a fire in the great stove halfway down the aisle, and the church grew quite warm. Sally Day wasn't paying much attention to the sermon, for she was more interested in the worshippers. She was feeling more and more confidant she was going to get along well with these people. Why, they seemed just as open and friendly as Marylanders! She took off her mantilla and laid it across her lap.

Mr. Horne happened to glance her way, and frowned and said something to his wife. She turned and whispered to Sally Day, "Mr. Horne asks you to cover up your gold pin."

Astonished, Sally Day looked at her father-in-law. He stared straight ahead. She hesitated a long time, but finally draped her mantilla over the pin. She didn't understand and she was offended, but her common sense told her that plumb in the middle of the sermon was not the time to argue.

The minister was talking about tolerance and patience as Christian virtues. The gentle minister Sally Day had listened to in Chesapeake City had never talked as directly to his people as the Revered Otis Crawford was doing. Mr. Crawford pointed out how necessary it was for everyone to be tolerant during these troubled, postwar days. He glanced along the rows of faces, and Sally Day guessed he was recollecting how grievously some of his own flock had suffered, for his eyes lingered when they came to the Hornes. He remarked that tolerance was easier to speak of than practice sometimes, but that time would help to heal the bitterness. He quoted Mr. Lincoln, "With charity for all, with malice towards none."

Sally Day observed her father-in-law's profile, noted with a shiver how it looked as though it was carved out of granite. Then she thought, It's bad enough to have a son killed in battle, but it's worse to know he died slowly of starvation when a few crusts of bread could have saved him. She remembered how her own Charles had looked, just skin and bones, when he had come to Chesapeake City after being released from Belle Isle. He had given what crusts he could beg or steal to his brother, but Ben had been racked by fever and dysentery, unable to fight off the death that stalked the prison.

She thought humbly that maybe Mr. Horne was entitled to his hate. Mr. Crawford's right, time will help, so I'll try to be nice and quiet and give Charles's father a chance to forget that I come from the South.

After another prayer the choir in the loft led the final hymn. Sally Day joined in heartily in her high soprano. The congregation started to file out, and the minister was waiting at the door. He greeted the Hornes respectfully, then clasped Sally Day's hand in both his warm ones, smiling down at her. "You're the new bride," he said. "Welcome to Connecticut, my dear."

He introduced his wife, standing next to him. Charlotte Crawford, blonde and rosy cheeked, leaned forward and kissed Sally Day who blurted out, "Why, you're not much older than I am."

Mrs. Crawford's laughter rang out. "I'm nineteen, Sally Day, but I'm an old, married woman with two bairns at home."

They were holding up the others and Charles nudged Sally Day along, but the Crawfords didn't let her go. "I could hear your voice in the hymns," Mrs. Crawford said. "It's rarely sweet and strong, and we'd love to have you join our choir."

"I'd be honored," Sally Day agreed happily.

"We'll call on you this week. Wednesday's our calling day," the minister announced, before he turned to his next parishioner.

The congregation lingered in the churchyard, chattering and gossiping while the children played tag among them, joyous in the strong sunshine. Mr. Horne marched his wife off and put her in the surrey, but so many people came up to be introduced to Charles's new bride, they delayed Charles and Sally Day.

Finally Mr. Horne threaded his way down the street full of buggies and surries. Sally Day couldn't keep her pleasure to herself. "I declare I never met a friendlier lot of people! I'm afraid I won't keep their names straight. And what a lovely minister! His wife said she had bairns at home, so is she Scottish? It'll be a pleasure to entertain them on Wednesday."

Charles looked so miserable, she glanced at his parents to find the reason. Their backs were ramrod stiff. Sally Day thought of Mrs. Horne as the peace-maker in the family, but now she was the one who said bitterly, "That young man needs correcting. He looked straight at us when he was prating of tolerance."

"He spoke to all, Mother," Charles said gently.

Sally Day saw then that a tear was sliding down Mrs. Hornes's gaunt cheek. She longed to reach over and put her arms around the older woman, but didn't dare.

Mrs. Horne wasn't through. "Talking of loving our enemies is just foolishness when they watched and rejoiced to see our boys die!"

Sally Day knew it was unusual for them to discuss Ben's death. "I was there, Mother," Charles said, "I was with Ben, and I've told you before it was the fever that killed him as much as the hunger."

His words hung on the air. Sally Day wanted to cry, seeing how hard it was for them to discuss the loss of their younger son.

Mr. Horne harshly cleared his throat. "I don't say we're not right," he said in a low voice. "We're entitled to our hate. But maybe Charles is right, too. The war is over and we've got to live with our loss and not nurse and cherish our bitter feelings. In any case, we're duty bound to entertain the minister and his wife. Maybe he meant no harm with his sermonizing, Elizabeth."

"I'm in no mood to entertain anybody," Mrs. Horne said stiffly.

"We have no choice, Elizabeth. He is the servant of the Lord."

A cloud had come over the bright day. For the rest of the day Sally Day tried to efface herself. She took off her black silk when she saw that Mrs. Horne had changed into her usual calico, and put away the brooch that seemed to bother Mr. Horne. She helped with dinner and with the washing up, and when evening came she fed the hens and scrubbed the milk cans for the men before they went out to milk the herd. She was trying to take over some of the heavy work, to lighten her mother-in-law's load.

She couldn't stay subdued very long at a time, however, and by the time they were sitting around the lamp in the kitchen after supper, she had bounced back to her usual cheerful self. She asked if the Crawfords would be staying for supper on Wednesday, and what kind of a party the Hornes would prepare in their honor.

"They'll come for tea," Mrs. Horne told her.

"Yes, but they might stay on," Sally Day said confidently. "Why, at home sometimes folks come for tea and stay for supper, and then they spend the night, and before you know it they've stayed a week!"

""Nothing like that will happen, I can promise you," Mrs. Horne said. "They'll come for tea, it'll be served in the parlor, and they'll stay one hour."

It worked out exactly that way.

Sally Day had not seen the Hornes' front parlor, and when she and her mother-in-law opened it on Wednesday morning to air it out, she was distressed. "It's cold in here," she protested.

"Of course it's cold. It's never used except for funerals and ministers' visits."

"Why do the shades have to be kept drawn?"

"To save the carpet, child. Does your mother leave the shades up so the sun fades your carpet?"

"Yes, she does," Sally Day admitted.

Velvet-covered chairs occupied each corner. Severe ancestors frowned down from the walls out of massive frames. Precisely in the middle was set a piecrust mahogany table, and precisely in its center rested a large Bible. High on a bookshelf, some bright-feathered stuffed birds perched on a branch under a glass bell.

Mrs. Horne handed Sally Day a dust cloth and she went through the motions of dusting, although she doubted that any dirt would dare filter into this austere room.

She took her time as she went along the rows of books, for she loved to read. She discovered that most of them were books of sermons. The most worn one, which was probably the liveliest, was Fox's "Book of Martyrs."

This room really scared Sally Day and she said, "Let's do

differently this time, Mrs. Horne, and give the Crawfords their tea in the kitchen. It's bright and warm and cheery there."

Her mother-in-law only answered, "The minister is always entertained in the front parlor."

Sally Day knew in her heart that the party was going to be a failure even before it started. She washed the pink-sprigged china which was only used for the minister, and watched her mother-in-law bake the golden pound cake which was always served to the minister. She buttered thin slices of bread and filled a silver compote with jam, as she was directed. But she was so positive the Crawfords would enjoy their tea more in the cheerful kitchen, she took her case to the men when they came in for dinner.

Mr. Horne heard her out but put an end to the argument in short order. "Ministers are always kept in the parlor. It's Mrs. Horne's house, so I guess we'll do as she sees fit."

Yes, it was Mrs. Horne's house and with each passing day Sally Day longed more passionately for her own house. Even if it was a cottage with a single room it would be her own. She let Mr. Horne's reminder pass, though, because his first remark tickled her funny bone. "Mr. Crawford sounds like a pet parrot kept in the parlor!" she pointed out.

Nobody smiled and she subsided. She did succeed, though, in sneaking a vase of goldenrod and purple asters into the cold funereal room.

At three o'clock the Hornes were ready and dressed in their Sunday best and precisely at three the minister's buggy drew up and he handed his wife down on the carriage stone. Apparently the parlor was no surprise to them. Everyone but Sally Day seemed to know how such a party ought to be conducted. The tea tray was brought in and set on the

table and Sally Day's gay bouquet of wild flowers was un-
ceremoniously banished. The tea was poured, the bread
and butter and cake were passed. Before anyone took a sip
Mr. Crawford said grace.

The conversation was as stiff as the furniture. Mr. Horne
and Mr. Crawford discussed church business, which had
something to do with the carriage shed's needing a new
roof. Pretty Mrs. Crawford asked for the recipe for the
gold cake, and Mrs. Horne wrote it out for her. Distressed,
Sally Day tried to introduce a few light remarks, and they
fell flat, although the callers smiled helpfully.

They'll never come again, Sally Day thought. They seem
so nice, but I'll never see them again.

They thanked their hosts politely for the hospitality.
Then, just as they were leaving, Charlotte Crawford turned
directly to Ezra Horne. She seemed a little afraid of what
she was going to say. She looked him straight in the eyes
and said, "Your daughter-in-law has a lovely voice, Mr.
Horne, and we need her in the choir. Choir practice is held
every Thursday evening. I hope you'll let her come." She
sounded a little defiant, as though she expected a refusal
and didn't intend to accept it.

"I don't hold with all the music your husband has put in
the service," Mr. Horne answered. "You know that, Mrs.
Crawford."

"Others like it," she replied bravely.

Her husband came to her rescue. "I hope you'll like it
too, Mr. Horne, when you get used to it. The Bible says,
'Make a joyful noise unto the Lord.' We are trying to make
a joyful noise on Sundays, and we'd like Sally Day's help if
she'd care to join in."

"I'd simply adore it!" Sally Day cried fervently.

They all watched Mr. Horne. He apparently decided not to go against the Bible, for he said grudgingly, "Very well, she can come."

"We want Charles, too, of course, for we need his bass. I've asked him before, but he couldn't see his way to coming to practice. Now he owes it to us to share his pretty wife with us," the minister said smoothly.

Formal goodbyes were said at the door, but Sally Day ran after the callers and took Charlotte's hand and pressed it, whispering, "Oh, thank you, thank you! You don't know it but you've just about saved my life!"

Chapter Eleven

I N EARLY OCTOBER Connecticut burst into flame as Charles had promised it would, and it was just as beautiful as he had predicted. Sugar maples turned every hue from yellow to garnet, laying a patchwork of color on the low hills. Fields shimmered like gold and Virginia creeper twisted like living fire up the trunks of trees. Purple asters and red sumac turned the road into a royal way.

Sally Day was absolutely bowled over by this sudden rush of splendor accompanied by flawless blue skies. In the weeks she had lived in Charles's home she had tried hard to be meek, helping with the heavy work and shutting herself up for hours in the dark downstairs room where the carding and weaving were done. Now that discipline was forgotten. She just couldn't stay indoors. When Mrs. Horne sent her out to feed the chickens or handed her the heavy pail of garbage for the hogs, her feet carried her off of their own volition. She found herself trotting along the road to see what new colors had been splashed over the landscape. She wandered off to look at her and Charles's land, leaned over the stone wall and dreamed of the house they would build there.

"Some people have spring fever but I reckon I've got a

real bad dose of fall fever," she apologized to her mother-in-law, one afternoon when she had been gone for hours.

Duke, who worshipped her, watched the door for her to emerge, and when she took off he took off, too. He was having a belated puppyhood, never having enjoyed one when he was young. He barked and frisked around her, taking the hem of her skirt gingerly in his teeth and looking up to her with laughing eyes. He also forgot his duties, and on one occasion when four-thirty came and he was supposed to be fetching the cows back to the barn he failed to show up. He and Sally Day were running in the thin woods, playing among the slender birches.

Charles and his father were engaged in spreading manure over the fields. Eighty acres were under cultivation, and the job of covering them was a back-breaking one. They worked from dawn to dark, and when they came in at night, bone tired, they smelled of manure. One evening Sally Day made the mistake of wrinkling her nose at her husband and telling him how he smelled.

This time it was he, not his parents, who pointed out to her the error of her ways. He waited until they went up to their room and then shut the door, because they had a tacit agreement they would never quarrel in front of other people. Probably he was only very tired, but he sounded like an old man when he said, "You've got no right to run off with the dog and keep him from his job. What's the matter with you? Lately you act as though you'd lost your wits."

She was ready to fire back at him, but then she saw how his shoulders sagged from exhaustion, how deep were the lines carved in his face. The work was too heavy for two men; the loss of Ben put too big a burden on his brother. Sally Day caught back the sharp remarks she longed to make, and said, "I'm sorry, Charles. I'll try to act my age."

This was on a Thursday evening, a choir practice night. Sally Day had hauled the tin bathtub up to their bedroom, planning to carry all the water so Charles could bathe. Now he sank back on the bed, his arm over his eyes. She said, "I reckon you're too tired to go to choir practice, dearest."

"I guess I am," he said. "If you'll let me off this once, Sally Day, I'll go next time."

"We know the song, anyway. We can sing on Sunday just the same."

He smiled wearily, grateful for her understanding. "The hard work will soon be over," he said. "Once cold weather comes, life will be easier. Right now Pa and I are hard pressed to get the land ready for its winter sleep."

"When winter comes do the good times begin?" she asked wistfully.

"What do you mean?"

"I mean parties and things in the town."

This was evidently a brand-new notion to him. "I don't know. I haven't any idea what goes on in town."

"But surely you and your brother went to parties!"

"No."

"Not a few times at least? Not once?"

"No. My folks don't hold with such things."

She didn't argue. She fetched the water and filled the tub and let him have his bath in peace. She was thinking of Ben, who had died at eighteen without ever learning about parties and light-hearted good times.

Her own birthday came later that month, but it was a very quiet occasion. Charles gave her a rope of twisted strands of gold. She had sometimes wondered if the Hornes were poor, but now she guessed they weren't, for this was a lavish gift. Her own parents sent her a hood of deep red-velvet, to go with her winter cloak. Mr. and Mrs. Horne ignored the fact that she had turned seventeen that day.

Sally Day was hurt, remembering all the parties at home, the cakes and presents and kisses for the birthday child. Charles saw she was hurt, and she could see how hard it was for him to have to explain that his parents thought that celebrating a birthday was a heathenish custom.

She tried to help him out. "Perhaps they're right," she said. "Anyway, I'm seventeen now and too old for such fripperies."

The leaves fell suddenly in a night. One day the trees were brave with color, and then a belated nor'easter struck and the next day their lovely clothes lay in tatters on the ground. Branches moved black and bare against the autumn sky.

Sally Day wrote Molly though, how it had been. "You have never seen anything so beautiful in your life as the Horne farm when October came," she told her. Then, because Molly liked stories of social goings-on, Sally wrote an account of choir practice and the mild little parties that followed, where light collations were served. "Winter's the lively time here," she wrote. "All sorts of parties, I expect, and I'll be the belle of the ball because I'm still the newest girl in town. Do you know that hereabouts, girls don't usually marry until they're twenty, or even twenty-one or two? My goodness, we'd think we were old maids already, wouldn't we?"

Molly answered, giving her the news of Chesapeake City. Tillman was a student at Harvard now, and planned to study law. Molly predicted that Tillman might stop off sometime on his way to Boston to visit Sally Day, to find out how she was making out as an old married woman. Molly's bits and pieces of news about all the cousins and aunts and uncles made Sally Day feel better, let her realize that Jericho wasn't thousands of miles away from Maryland, as it often seemed.

Sometimes, now that the days were getting so short and the landscape was so empty, homesickness settled on her like an evil cloud, and she had a hard time fighting it off.

Lacey White Wyatt wrote, too, but her letter wasn't long and newsy, it was short and not sweet. "I hope you are well," she had the grace to say. Then she went on, "Perhaps the enclosed will prove to you what's going on in the South nowadays and will open your eyes to the fact that all the Yankees up north are not angels."

Sally felt a hot flush of resentment. Then she read the enclosures and understood that Lacey White's indignation was a righteous one. She had sent along a letter from a South Carolina relative of hers who was also a distant cousin of Sally Day's. Included were clippings from a South Carolina newspaper. Sally Day was appalled to learn how northern carpetbaggers had invaded the South and were oppressing and cheating the citizens. The news stories gave instances of cruel, dishonest dealings with old people, with helpless women widowed by the war.

At first Sally Day thought, Oh dear, I wish Lacey White hadn't written me, I'd rather not know. Then she remembered her father saying once that it was better to be aware of evil than to be ignorant, because then you could do something about it.

Lacey White ended her letter with the remark, "Maybe your Mr. Lincoln you were so fond of would have handled things differently but you'll pardon me if I doubt it."

Lacey White was getting even with Sally Day because the George Hammond side of the family had been on the Union side, the winning side. She was also retaliating because Sally Day had chosen to marry a Yankee instead of Lacey White's own brother. Sally Day knew this. Yet that sentence of Lincoln's rang in her head, "With malice towards none, with charity for all." Why couldn't the victorious North show kindness to the beaten foe, at least to the helpless ones? It could well afford to.

Hot with indignation, because after all it was her own people who were suffering, Sally Day carried the letter and newspaper to the supper table. She didn't mean to start a ruckus, she just thought the Hornes ought to know.

Charles had been pleased he was able to bring Sally Day mail from home when he came back from town, and now he asked, "Did you have a good letter from your cousin, Sally Day?"

"No, not exactly," she told him. "Lacey White sent news from another cousin of ours in South Carolina."

"You have relatives in the deep south?" Mr. Horne asked.

"Oh, my goodness yes, I've got relatives all over the South, we're a big family. Anyway, Cousin Ellie in Charleston sent some horrible stories about the carpetbaggers who've gone down there. Here, I'll read you bits and pieces."

Charles tried to stop her. "Sally Day, let's get on with our supper."

"I'll read while you have yours. I'm too upset to eat." Sally Day proceeded to relate how the Northern speculators had descended "like a swarm of locusts," as the newspaper said, and were spreading misery through the South. She concluded with Lacey White's remark about the martyred Lincoln.

Then at last she looked around. Maybe Mrs. Horne's narrow face looked as though it was carved from stone, but Mr. Horne's was black with rage. "Those are cheap lies!" he thundered.

Sally Day was scared by his anger but she didn't back down. "That's probably not rightly so, sir. We knew we could trust Mr. Lincoln, but we don't know about those folks who are in power, now he's dead."

"Sally Day, you're only a woman, and these affairs are beyond your understanding," Charles warned.

That was certainly the wrong thing to say, for Sally Day had grown up in a home where women's opinions were respected. She told her husband, "They're not over my head, and I've got a right to be upset! Mr. Lincoln would feel terrible to have such things happening. He was a good, kind man. That's why we loved him!"

"How can you say that?" Mrs. Horne broke in. "The people of Maryland hated the President!"

Sally Day's mouth fell open in surprise. "Didn't you know my father was a Union man? Lots of my folks were for the Union!"

Silence greeted this. She asked, "Don't you believe me?"

Charles tried to help her out then. "I thought I'd made it clear that Sally Day's parents weren't Secesh," he told his mother.

Sally Day knew she had been a fool. She should never have brought the letter down, she should have remembered how severely the Hornes had suffered from the war. She was in a mess now. She couldn't back down, however. She had to go on, and she began quietly, "I want to tell you about the day my Papa took us all to Baltimore to pay our respects to the President."

Not one detail of that long day had faded from her memory. It was as clear as if it had happened the day before. She started with the trip in the crowded train, filled with Maryland folk who wanted to honor the President. She told of the night in the hotel, of the silent pall which had hung over Baltimore. She described the next morning, how the rain had come down so you couldn't tell whether people's faces were wet with rain or tears, as they struggled to reach the railroad station. She was seeing again the black hearse, the horses shiny with rain, the drooping plumes and mourning drapery.

The Hornes stared at her across the table, but she was too intent on remembering to try to read their faces. They were listening to every word, anyway. They followed as she told of the silent march through the streets to the Exchange Building, the churchbells tolling, the cannon thundering, the sound of scuffling feet.

She pictured Lincoln's still face against the satin pillow, and cried again remembering that heart-shaking moment.

"And then we went back to the station," she said simply. "We were swept along with the thousands who wanted to stay near the President as long as they could. Mrs. Lincoln carried the coffin of her child back to Illinois, too. That was their son Willie, and my sister Wilhelmina cried something awful because she's called Willie, too. My brother Eugene howled along with her, but turned out he was hungry. We had forgotten all day long about eating."

She tucked her damp handkerchief in her cuff, and said quietly, "The next time you folks start thinking of me as a Southern sympathizer and one of those who looked with favor on the killing of Northern boys, just remember, please, I was one of those who paid my last respects to Mr.

Lincoln. It wasn't always easy to be loyal to the Union when you lived in Maryland, and were torn in both directions. There was wrong and right on both sides, and cruelty and kindness, too. I know a little of what I'm talking about."

With that Sally Day snatched up her shawl from its nail near the door, and ran outside. Charles came after her. He simply put his arms around her and held her, and she buried her face in his shoulder. She didn't mind that he smelled of the barn, it was just the Charles smell that she loved.

Finally she raised her head. "I've wrecked everything," she said. "Oh, Charles, I don't know what to do. They'll never love me now."

He rested his cheek on top of her head and said quietly, "Every day I learn something new about you."

"And tonight you've learned that I haven't got a single little old brain in my head."

"No. That's not exactly what I found out tonight." Charles held her in silence. Then he went on, "I hope you've learned something, too, darling, from what happened tonight. My folks aren't just twisted and ugly inside, the way they may seem sometimes. They're lonely inside, that's their trouble, both of them, both Ma and Pa. Now let's go back in. It's cold and you're shivering."

"Charles, I can't face them."

He chuckled deep in his throat and said, "Sometimes I suspect that if you met a lion you'd face it down somehow." They walked back arm in arm.

Mr. Horne was raking the dead clinkers out of the kitchen range. Sally Day went straight to him. "Mr. Horne, I'm apologizing for my boldness in challenging you."

He said without turning around, "That was quite a story you told us, Sarah." She waited. Finally he said, "You told it well."

After that night Sally Day sensed that her situation had altered. She wasn't just a stranger on a visit, or the flibbety-gibbet their son had brought home as a souvenir of the war. She was different from them so she was set apart, but in some new way she belonged.

There was no change in the others though that she could really put her finger on, and certainly Sally Day herself didn't change. One night when she and Charles were alone in their room, he happened to mention casually that if things worked out all right he might start thinking about building their own house in the spring. He would help his father through the plowing and heavy work, but after the tobacco had been set and the corn and rye planted, he would make a start on digging the cellar hole. The neighbors would give him a hand, cutting the timbers and raising the frame.

"You mean we'd have a raising party!" Sally Day cried rapturously.

Charles sounded discouraged. "Sally Day, I just begin to think you're growing up and then I find out your mind's been on parties the whole livelong time!"

"That's right," Sally Day answered. "When I'm ninety years old I'll still be thinking up excuses for stirring things up and having a good time!"

Chapter Twelve

SOMETIMES THINGS WERE better and sometimes worse. But the worse was better than it had been at the beginning, Sally Day thought philosophically.

At least she was getting so she could manage her spells of homesickness now. Her mother's gay, loving letters didn't send her to her bedroom for an hour of moping as they had first done. She could write her mother now without longing to pour out her troubles. She was very glad she had never given in to the impulse to tell how difficult Charles's parents were. Now she knew they were not in the least wicked, they were only cold. Coldness was their nature, not something directed against her.

There were several kinds of cold, she discovered. The kind the thermometer showed was an enemy everybody fought in this northern state. When December came and the cold weather really moved in, it was like a wolf eternally at the door. Sally Day thought she'd never be able to stand it, that the marrow of her bones would freeze solid.

During the first week of December they awakened one morning to discover the world had turned white. Wind was lashing the falling snow into storms that swirled around the corner of the barn and piled in drifts against the house.

Charles struggled out and dug a path to the barn. When he and his father returned to the house after milking the cows, Mr. Horne growled at Sally Day, "Gal, you look like you've inherited a million dollars."

She hadn't realized her pleasure in the storm showed that much. She said, "This is a real treat to an unreconstructed Southern gal like me, Mr. Horne!" Once in a while, lately, she joked with him this way.

He only said, "Hurrumph!"

Then her joy collapsed like a struck balloon, "Oh, dear, Charles was going to take me to town today to do the shopping!"

"It'll wait," her father-in-law said. "With the larder and root cellar full we won't starve."

After the chores were done, however, the men were free unless they looked around and made work for themselves. The snow stopped before noon and the sun broke through, turning the world into shimmering diamonds. Sally Day trotted from window to window, staring out longingly. Charles suggested, "It wouldn't do any great harm if we harnessed up the sleigh and went to town after all."

The horse Ebenezer and Sally Day were just about equally pleased to be flying along the road to town. Charles, enjoying her happiness, leaned down to kiss Sally's nose within the shelter of her velvet hood.

Ebenezer trotted smartly along Main Street, his bells jingling, and stopped in front of Strong's General Store. The men were gathered around the stove while their womenfolk shopped, and smiling faces turned to the door as the Hornes entered. We do make kind of a good-looking couple, Sally Day thought complacently.

Mr. Strong beckoned to Charles, "Come, give us your

opinion," he ordered. "The ladies are talking about putting on a big party for you veterans. The Jericho boys were included in the one Norwich gave last summer for the whole company, but we here would like to honor our own boys. How would you feel about it?"

"I guess it would be all right," Charles said.

Jane Cope, who was Sally Day's special friend in the choir, drew her into a circle of the women. "The Crawfords think it's a fine idea and will help," Jane said. "We want to have an evening party, and have it soon, next week maybe. That will make a right gay start for the holidays. Everybody in town is to be invited. Those who want to work on it will meet at the church this Sunday after service."

Charles could have no part in planning the celebration because he was to be a guest of honor along with the other boys Jericho had sent to war. On Sunday he drove his parents home after church, and then returned to town to wait for Sally Day while she attended the meeting.

She was glad to discover that Connecticut people knew how to give a party. The men promised to decorate the Town Hall and to hire a fiddler for the dancing that would follow the supper. The ladies were to take care of the refreshments.

Each of them suggested her own specialty, the kind of cake or pie or meat dish she made best. Sally Day told Mrs. Crawford, who was making out the list, "I'll bring cupcakes."

"What are they?" Jane asked.

"Why, they're the dearest little cakes you ever saw," Sally Day exclaimed. "My mother always fixes them for parties at home, and she taught me how."

"They're the newest thing," Mrs. Strong agreed. "My husband just laid in a supply of the tins you bake them in, but I haven't tried them yet."

The Hornes had just finished dinner when Sally Day and Charles reached home. Mr. Horne looked glum while Sally Day chattered on about the gala celebration which was being planned, but his wife seemed interested. She even agreed that she and Mr. Horne might attend it. Apparently they had discussed this, and Sally Day realized it was a very great concession on their part.

"That would be lovely," Sally Day said. "You and I can make cupcakes together. I promised three dozen of them."

"What do you make them in?" Mrs. Horne asked.

"Cupcake tins. Mr. Strong stocks them at his store, so we'll buy a dozen."

"They may be expensive," Mrs. Horne warned.

"Oh, now they're just little old tin cups, they couldn't cost much."

They did, though. When Charles went to town the next morning he brought one home and reported it had cost fifty cents. "We'll get along with a half dozen and use them over and over," Sally Day said.

Then her father-in-law unexpectedly put his back up and turned stubborn. Evidently he didn't like the idea of the party anyhow, and considered cupcakes just a flighty notion Sally Day had brought North with her. "Six of the useless things will cost three dollars. We'll drop that idea," he announced.

"But I can't. I've promised," Sally Day protested.

"It doesn't matter what you've promised. Money's too hard to come by to throw it away. You can make an ordinary cake or pie for this affair."

Sally Day said no more, for his tone discouraged argument. But her mind was made up. She had promised to bring cupcakes, and bring cupcakes she would.

The grand affair was to take place on Friday. On Thursday morning Sally Day was dressed and downstairs at dawn, poking up the fire. If she was going to bake thirty-six cupcakes one at a time, she was going to have a busy day.

She spent the entire day washing the tin, greasing it, filling it halfway with batter, putting it into the oven for fifteen minutes, taking out the cake and washing the tin for the next one. By noon her back was ready to break from leaning into the oven. She noticed that her father-in-law watched her with the strange twist on his lips that was his kind of a smile, and realized he expected her to give up. Charles fussed at her because she was gettting so tired, and Mrs. Horne said, distressed, "Give it up, Sarah, and let me piece out your little cakes with a gold cake."

"No, thank you just the same," Sally Day said, and wearily plodded to the sink to wash the small tin for what seemed like the hundredth time.

At six o'clock she turned out the thirty-sixth cupcake on the bread board. Each one was spongy and moist and exactly the right golden brown, and she surveyed her work with satisfaction. "After supper it'll be kind of fun decorating them," she chatted on. "But, my goodness, I hope I get my back straightened out before tomorrow evening, or I won't be in any condition for the dancing."

There was a silence in the room which deepened. Mr. Horne finally broke it. "They're planning to have dancing at this affair?"

"Yes. Jane Cope says the fiddler they've hired is just wonderful."

"Oh, dear," Mrs. Horne said softly.

"We won't be there to find out whether he's good or not,"

her husband said.

"Why? What do you mean?" Sally Day asked. She was just too exhausted to be tactful or try to cajole her father-in-law.

"None of mine will go where there's any dancing, for it's the devil's invention."

"But we've got to go," Sally Day said. "The party's in honor of Charles and the other boys. And I promised to bring the cakes, and besides, I'm going to wear my blue silk with the fringe!"

"You can send the cakes, since you promised them, but you and your blue silk and its fringe and the rest of us are staying home and there won't be one more word about it."

And there wasn't. He stood there like a piece of granite in the kitchen. The look Sally Day gave him was pure hatred but he stared straight back into her eyes. Mrs. Horne didn't try to move him and neither did Charles.

Caught in the middle once again between his parents and his wife, Charles sided with his parents this time. "It's Pa's principle and he's head of this household," he told Sally Day miserably. "I'm sorry but that's the way it is. If I'd heard there was going to be dancing I'd have warned you. You can't move my father on this point. Anybody who dances has taken the first step on the road to hell; that's what he believes, and you'll never change him."

All night long Sally Day lay stiffly beside her husband, too exhausted and too hot with anger to sleep. Charles's body was just as rigid.

In the morning she iced the cakes, packed them carefully, and ordered Charles to make the best explanation he could to the committee as to why the Hornes wouldn't be there. She didn't care what he told them but hoped it would come close to the truth, that his father was a bigoted old man who hated to see people having a good time.

Mr. Horne was the head of the house, she added, so she would honor and obey him. But that didn't mean she had to like him.

"Sally Day, Sally Day," Charles groaned, "when are you going to grow up?"

"Never!" Sally Day snapped back, her face a mask of fury.

Chapter Thirteen

SALLY DAY DIDN'T bounce back very well from that defeat. Up until then she had cherished the notion that she was winning her father-in-law over, that in time she would cajole him and turn him into a nice human being. Now she felt she had lost a real battle, and furthermore she felt she no longer cared whether he turned into a nice human being or not.

What made everything worse was that Christmas was coming on fast. She received a letter from her father, a rare event for he wasn't much of a letter writer. "Dearest daughter," he wrote, "please don't be angry because your Daddy enclosed ten dollars along with his love. I know that your husband takes good care of you and provides for all your wants, but I also know that at Christmas time a woman needs a little extra money in her purse, and no questions asked how she spends it.

"Your old home will be the poorer during this holiday season because we will miss you here. We will make merry but we'll wish you were here. Your new home will be the richer because of your happy spirit, and that's the way the world goes and it's right and proper. Daughters have to make their own lives, and we don't begrudge Charles and his parents your gaiety. Will you convey to your husband our affection and to Mr. and Mrs. Horne our respectful greetings?"

He ended, "Your loving father." Then below came a scribbled line, "Dear little girl, will you come and visit us in the new year?"

That last question had her father's tender heart in it. The money was welcome and Sally Day was glad to have it, but the love her father sent her across the miles was the treasure she cherished.

She had a box of gifts ready to mail to the Maryland folks, small things she had made herself, a tea cozy for her mother and handkerchiefs edged with lace for Willie and cousin Molly. She had purchased at Mr. Strong's store an iron penny bank for Gene and a new pipe for her father. She hastily scrawled a note to her father, thanking him for his gift, promising she would be home for a visit in the spring. Loyalty to her husband made her leave out her longing for Maryland, her dread of the long winter ahead in the Hornes' house.

Since her disappointment about missing the dance, Charles had acted almost humbly eager to please her. Sometimes his humility bothered her. It wasn't his fault his father was a crabbed old man bent on spoiling other people's happiness. At other times it gave her a perverse satisfaction to see him acting like an eager puppy dog. Today when she announced at dinnertime that she wanted to go to town, to mail her package and do a little shopping, he leaped at the idea. "I'll gladly drive you in," he said, although as Sally Day knew he had planned to spend the afternoon helping his father haul logs from the woodlot.

A warm spell had taken all the snow, and the road had

thawed. The buggy lurched along in the muddy ruts, throwing Sally Day against her husband. She tried to sit stiffly upright. They hardly spoke. Sally Day stared morosely over the bleak, brown countryside, wondering how in heaven's name she had ever convinced herself there was anything beautiful about Connecticut.

Charles drew up before the store and helped her down, telling her he would mail her letter and package. He reached in his pocket for the money for her shopping. It gave Sally Day real pleasure to be able to say, "No, thank you, Charles, I have money of my own."

"But you're not supposed to spend the money your father gave you as your wedding gift."

"I'm not. He sent me some more in a letter."

Her husband scowled. "Does he think I can't take care of my own wife?"

"Oh no, nothing like that, Charles," Sally Day said sweetly. "He just did it because he knows every woman likes a little extra at holiday time."

"If you'd asked me I'd have provided whatever you wanted."

Instead of patting his arm and thanking him, as a good wife would have done, Sally Day simply let the matter drop. "I reckon I'll be ready to go home in about an hour," she told him.

She had seen no signs of Christmas preparations in the Horne house, and had no idea whether they planned to celebrate the day at all. *Just the same I'm going to celebrate it,* she had promised herself. Now her father's gift made it possible for her to do it in style.

Stout, motherly Mrs. Strong was behind the dry-goods counter. It warmed Sally Day's heart, the way the men sit-

ting around the stove beamed when she walked in. One
sang out, "You're looking mighty pert today, Mis' Horne!"

"I feel mighty pert," she told him, giving him the radiant
kind of smile she hadn't bestowed on her husband for several days.

She confided her plans to Mrs. Strong. "I'd like a nice
lace collar for my mother-in-law. I reckon Mrs. Horne's
calicos could do with a bit of sprucing up, and I want real
French lace if you've got it, Mrs. Strong. Also, I reckon a
pair of bright red suspenders might do the same for Mr.
Horne. Don't you think so?"

Mrs. Strong burst into laughter. "Oh, land, child," she
said, "wait until it gets around town you gave Ezra Horne
red suspenders! He never buys anything livelier than black."

Sally Day was feeling more cheerful by the minute and
said gaily, "Whether he wears them or not, it's good for a
man to own one pair of red suspenders."

"And what about Charles?"

Sally Day stopped smiling. Charles's gift was a serious
matter. Regardless of the fact that she was often angry
enough with him to hit him, and longed to leave him forever and hated him and his dark, brooding countenance,
she loved him so much she still trembled like a bride when-
ever he came near her, and she knew she would never, never
leave him as long as she lived. Maybe she couldn't sort out
how she really felt about him, but she knew she wanted to
buy him the finest present she could manage.

Mrs. Horne's French lace collar would cost around two
dollars, and one dollar was enough to spend for Mr. Horne's
suspenders. Also, Sally Day had resolved to buy Duke a
collar. He was only a country dog and had never owned
one, but he was her best friend on the farm and deserved to

be dressed as well as any town dog. That would cost another dollar, the same as Mr. Horne's gift. That left six dollars for Charles.

Mrs. Strong solved her problem by lifting out a box she kept under the counter. "I thought Mr. Strong made a mistake when he bought some French leather goods, the last time he went to New York," she explained. "I told him these were too elegant for Jericho."

The gloves she spread on the counter were a beautiful, fawn color kid, the softest Sally Day had ever felt. They were the kind a gentleman might purchase when he went to Europe. Sally Day looked inside, and sure enough, "Paris, France" was stamped there. "How much do they cost?" she asked.

"We should get more, but they might gather dust for years before anybody in Jericho makes up his mind he can afford them. I'll let you have them for five dollars."

Mrs. Strong hesitated and then added, "Are you sure Charles will wear them? He's a farmer."

Sally Day said, "It's a little like the suspenders for his father, Mrs. Strong, only it's different. Even if a farmer never puts them on, it's good for his soul to own a pair of gloves that came from Paris, France."

"I call that pretty good reasoning for a girl of your tender years," Mrs. Strong declared. She helped Sally Day wrap all the gifts in tissue and tucked them into her shopping poke.

Christmas Day came, and it was a quiet, pleasant day, and that was about all that could be said for it. Not one decoration was put up. Mrs. Horne did some extra baking, and that was all. Apparently the Hornes didn't keep up even one foolish, lovely custom. Sally Day figured out that

Mr. Horne lumped Christmas in with the other things he considered heathenish.

On Christmas Eve she had revolted briefly. The family had finished supper and was getting ready for bed when she put on her heavy cloak and opened the back door. Charles asked where she was going and she told him, "To the barn. They say the animals talk together while they're waiting for the Christ child on Christmas Eve, and I'm going out to see if it's true."

Ezra Horne looked shocked to the roots of his being. Charles lit the lantern for her and waited at the door. The real reason Sally Day had suggested going was because she wanted to get off by herself and cry, but when she walked into the barn she found she had lost her desire to weep.

Duke rushed to meet her, overjoyed, for he wasn't used to having visitors in the middle of the night. The chickens on the rafters, disturbed by the lantern, set up a sleepy clucking. Sally Day went along the line of cows, petting the noses and calling each by name.

The two work horses and Ebenezer whinneyed, leaning over their box stalls to greet her. Maybe the animals weren't talking among themselves as they were supposed to do, but they radiated dumb affection for a lonely girl. She thought as she closed the barn door behind her, I reckon I actually like the animals better than I do some people.

Charles's parents must have suspected she planned to give gifts for they had some ready. Mrs. Horne's was a new ironstone washbowl and pitcher, white china decorated with pink roses. Mr. Horne's showed a wry humor for it was a set of six cupcake tins. Was it an apology for the awful way he had acted about the dance? Charles's gift was a dozen pure linen handkerchiefs. He acted so anxious that she be pleased, she made a big fuss over all her presents.

Mr. Horne glowered when he opened his red suspenders. Sally Day was watching him. His face didn't exactly clear, but his mouth twisted wryly, as he realized she was teasing. He and Sally Day declared a truce then, for the rest of the day.

The parlor remained closed. No tree spread its green branches indoors, no Yule log blazed on the hearth, and worst of all no laughter rang through the still house, such as would be filling the Hammond house in Maryland that day. Sally Day respected the Hornes' mood, however, knowing they must be thinking of Ben, for this was their second Christmas without him.

They spoke so seldom of him, Sally Day had no idea what kind of boy Ben had been. She doubted, though, that even his presence could have lightened the heavy spirit of the Horne house, to work the special magic that was Christmas.

If Charles and I are blessed with children I'll make special days so bright and shining they'll carry the memory of them all their lives, she resolved. That was what her own parents had done for her. Maybe this made the day seem even gloomier when she experienced one that had no shine on it at all. Nevertheless, it was better to be disappointed than it was to have no real feeling for Christmas.

The last day of the year came, and the Hornes went to a candlelight service at the church. It was a simple service, just a few hymns and prayers, but it was beautiful. Instead of sitting stiffly in their pews the congregation formed a circle around the walls of the big room. A single large candle burned on the altar, and each person held a tall, white one. The minister lit his from the altar candle, then turned to his wife Charlotte who stood beside him, kissed her and lit her candle. This little ceremony went from one to the next, all around the room, until the circle of flickering lights was complete.

Charles lit his candle from his mother's. He turned to Sally Day and hugged her tight, and his eyes burned with love.

Since the first day she had arrived at his house, Sally Day had never once kissed her father-in-law. Now she lifted her face and he bent to kiss her, because he had no choice. She sensed that he was in a dark mood, but gave it little thought, for she was too moved by the solemnity of the service.

They sang another hymn, and Mr. Crawford made a few remarks about fellowship and loving one's neighbor. They finished with "Auld Lang Syne," and filed out of the church still carrying the candles.

They emerged into the cold, windy night. The sleigh ride home under the crisp stars, with the bells ringing and the runners singing on the frozen road, seemed like part of the same happy experience. Sally Day pressed close against Charles in the back seat, and he held her warmly against him.

When they reached home Mrs. Horne poked up the fire in the stove because they were all half frozen, and heated a kettle of soup. Sally Day took off her winter cloak and hood. She was wearing her red merino, and Charles could hardly take his eyes off her. Well, it was no news to Sally Day that the rich red of her merino put crimson in her cheeks. Still, it was a fine thing to see your husband's eyes kindle when he looked at you, especially if you were an old married woman of three months.

The spirit of fellowship they had brought home from church still lay like a spell on Sally Day, and when they were sitting around the table drinking the soup she declared, "That was the most beautiful ceremony I've ever seen."

Mrs. Horne murmured agreement, but glanced apprehensively up at her husband. His disapproval was so strong it was palpable in the air and although she knew it was foolish, Sally Day challenged him. "Don't you agree, Mr. Horne?"

"No," he said shortly.

Charles whispered, "Don't argue, Sally Day."

She obeyed him, only murmuring, "Well, I thought it was beautiful and I'm glad we went."

"It was pagan," her father-in-law stated. "Kissing and the lighting of candles have no place in the church. It was almost as bad as turning the Lord's house into a theatre."

Sally Day should have guessed that a person who disapproved of dancing would also disapprove of the theatre, lumping them in with gambling and drinking and other vices. She herself had been to the theatre twice, when traveling troupes of actors came to Elkton. She thoughtlessly remarked, "I never knew there was anything wicked about the theatre."

Mrs. Horne tried to stop what was happening. She gathered up the soup bowls, saying, "It's high time all of us were abed."

Sally Day was agreeable to that. She took the bowls from the older woman and started to rinse them under the pump. "Sarah, have you ever set foot inside a theatre?" Mr. Horne demanded.

"Yes, sir. Twice. My parents took me."

"They shouldn't have done that."

"I'm sorry, we all enjoyed it." Now Sally Day was angry, for Mr. Horne was criticising her parents, and that she couldn't allow. "Other folks don't see as you do, sometimes, Mr. Horne," she went on, keeping her voice even. "I know you admired Mr. Lincoln and you know he often went to see plays in Washington, and said it eased his mind and lightened his burdens. Why, I read in the paper he was laughing at what was going on on the stage that night at Ford's at the very moment the assassin fired the shot."

Mr. Horne growled, "If he'd set a good example and stayed away then he'd be alive today."

"That's not so. Booth would have sought him out and killed him somewhere else."

Charles stopped the argument before she could get any angrier by taking her arm and marching her upstairs to bed. That didn't calm her, though, and she went on sputtering, "Everybody's wrong except him. But he needn't go around saying President Lincoln was a wicked man. I know better!"

Charles sounded annoyed. "Why can't you ever pass up a chance to argue with Pa? Why don't you try to help us keep the peace?"

"Because that's not right," Sally Day declared. "Letting him think you agree with him is the worst way to encourage him. A person who holds ideas as wrong as his can do a lot of harm."

Chapter Fourteen

MRS. HORNE QUOTED, "When the days begin to lengthen, then the cold begins to strengthen." It was certainly true that January. The thermometer sank to ten below, then to twenty on one particularly bitter dawn. It sluggishly rose to a few degrees above zero by midafternoon. When dark came it sank again. The snow squeaked as Sally Day walked on it, and when she opened her mouth to take a breath her lungs ached like fire.

She had never experienced such savage cold, and even when she drew a chair up to the stove, wrapping her heavy skirts about her, she couldn't stop shivering. Charles worried, and his mother suggested, "Probably Sarah's blood is thinner because she comes from the South. Her blood will thicken up and then she'll be all right."

When they went up to bed at night they took soapstones which Mrs. Horne heated in the oven and wrapped in pieces of soft wool. The last thing she did was put hot coals in the brass bed warmer with the long handle and turn down the beds and iron the icy sheets. Despite the warmed sheets and the soapstone at her feet, Sally Day still continued to shiver in the deep feather bed.

Charles fussed at her, and Sally Day agreed she did feel

kind of awful. Her wavery mirror showed deep circles under her eyes. Mrs. Horne questioned her, and Sally Day admitted she didn't have any pain but she just didn't feel right. "If you don't improve soon, maybe you should see the doctor," her mother-in-law suggested.

Despite the bitter cold, Duke was left out all night in the barn. The cows were kept in their stalls when snow covered the meadows, and Charles assured Sally Day that all the animals kept warm. Their own body heat made the barn tolerable. Just the same, Sally Day couldn't help feeling concerned over homely, shaggy Duke. In her unhappy moments she sometimes thought of him as her best friend.

One afternoon he went off, and failed to show up when the men did the milking and locked the barn for the night. Sally Day had given Charles the dog's supper in a bowl, and Charles brought it back with him. When bedtime came Sally Day watched for a long time at the window, hoping to see Duke come trotting across the moonlit yard. Finally she obeyed her husband and went up to bed.

He slept heavily beside her, but she stayed awake listening. Finally she heard Duke's soft whine. He was too afraid of the humans in the house to make a real noise.

Sally Day slipped out of bed, wrapped her warm robe about her and pulled on her gaiters. She didn't need a candle, for moonlight streamed through the windows. She slid the bolt and turned the key.

Duke had bedded down in the snow right outside the door stone. He hesitated when she held the door wide, for this was the first time in his life that he had been invited into the house. She ordered him and he came.

He walked stiffly but seemed to be all right. She fetched his supper from the pantry, but he seemed more interested in licking her hands to show his gratitude. She pushed him down on the rug in front of the stove and warned him, "Keep quiet now. I'll try to get down before anybody else in the morning and let you out."

She closed the kitchen door. She heard the click of his toenails on the bare boards, then his soft snuffling as he tried to follow her. She went back and made him lie on the rug again, but each time she left him he scratched at the door.

"You're more trouble than you're worth," she scolded him. She couldn't put him out where he'd freeze to death, so finally she wrapped her heavy clock around her and lay down on the floor beside him. She figured on staying until he slept and then trying to sneak away. Instead, she fell sound asleep herself.

As ill luck would have it, Ezra Horne was the first one down the next morning. When he discovered his daughter-in-law asleep on the kitchen floor, her arms wrapped around the dog, he thundered at her, and his roar brought the others hurrying.

"Maybe it was foolish but no great harm's been done," his wife tried to calm him.

Charles saw nothing funny in the incident either. His reaction was that she preferred sleeping on the floor with the dog to her own bed, and his disapproving silence was just as bad as his father's all that day.

Why is it that everything I do turns out wrong? Sally Day wondered. She knew she'd made herself look silly in everyone's eyes. Would they ever look on her as a responsible young matron, entitled to the respect due a real wife?

Despite the bitter weather, Mr. Horne didn't even consider missing the regular January meeting of the church's

Board of Elders. It was his duty to go, that was enough for him. Charles offered to drive him, but his father wouldn't listen to that. Although the road hadn't been rolled he was sure Ebenezer could make it through the drifts.

To Sally Day, an evening without the presence of the head of the house was a real treat. She felt easier, lately, with her mother-in-law. Since September Mrs. Horne had slowly warmed toward her, and nowadays there was little strain between them. They weren't friends exactly, for friendship implied talking and sharing, but Sally Day was deeply happy to see that their silent companionship meant a great deal to Charles's mother.

Several days had gone by since Sally Day had been caught sleeping on the floor with the dog. She was beginning to recover her old gaiety.

Did the others welcome Mr. Horne's absence? Wild horses would never drag such an admission from them, Sally Day knew, but just the same Charles and his mother seemed uncommonly cheerful. Sally Day was learning to darn her husband's knitted socks, and they got to laughing about the size of the holes. Mrs. Horne mixed up a batch of brown-sugar candy and Charles cracked hickory nuts and picked out the meats for her. The mantel clock struck ten and Mrs. Horne exclaimed, "I declare, I don't know where this evening's gone, it went so fast!"

"Maybe that's because we were having a good time," Sally Day suggested.

They heard the scraping on the sleigh's runners on the stones in the lane. Mrs. Horne pushed the teakettle onto the hot part of the stove, preparing to fix her husband a cup of soup.

He looked grim and pleased, both at once, when he came

in stamping the snow off his boots. "How did your meeting go, Mr. Horne?" Sally Day asked brightly.

"Pretty well, girl."

He took the cup his wife handed him and said "Thank you," two words that didn't often come from his lips. "Yes, pretty well," he said, "though the outcome may not satisfy everybody. It looks like the Reverend Crawford will be leaving Jericho."

They stared at him. "Why?" Charles asked. "Has he had an offer from another church?"

"No, but in all probability he won't be invited to stay for another year. Not everybody favors him and his ways."

"I don't understand. Why, everybody loves Otis and Charlotte Crawford!" Sally Day exclaimed.

"There, you've put your finger on one thing some of us don't favor," Mr. Horne said. "The minister and his wife ought to hold themselves above the congregation and not get so friendly that folks feel free to call them by their first names."

Charles sounded troubled. "Did the Board definitely decide to let him go?"

"The formal vote was postponed until next month's meeting, but the sense of tonight's meeting was that he's too young for our church, and his ways are not ours. There were others besides myself who took offense at the way he conducted that New Year's Eve service, for instance. Candles and all that claptrap."

"I just don't believe it," Sally Day said flatly. "They're the nicest couple I ever met, and all the young people love them!"

"It's just as well there aren't any young people on the Board of Elders, then. A minister's supposed to be looked up to, not loved."

"I don't like it," Charles said.

That caught Sally Day by surprise. For months she had been longing to hear him disagree with his father. Something told her to keep silent now, to let Charles be the one to fight the minister's cause.

"It doesn't matter whether you like it or not," his father said. "You don't vote on the Board of Elders."

No more was said that night, and there was little discussion in the days that followed. Charles went around with a troubled face, and Sally Day could sense in him a growing opposition to his father. The young people went as usual to choir practice, and all the Hornes attended church on Sunday. Sally Day guessed that the minister knew what was afoot, for he rarely smiled, but Charlotte was her usual cheerful self, so perhaps her husband had not told her.

It was so terribly unfair! Sally Day longed to organize a battle, to hold meetings and get a petition signed, to do something, anything that would stop what the elders planned. She suggested this to Charles and he advised, "Hold off, Sally Day. You're a newcomer and you might do more harm than good. A lot of the other young fellows feel as you and I do, and are meeting to discuss it. That's why it took me so long to get home from town the other day."

Then, in the middle of the month, there came a new development that was so world-shaking it almost pushed the Crawfords and their troubles out of Sally Day's mind.

As the wintry January days dragged on she continued to be plagued with vague feelings of malaise. Sometimes it was very hard for her to pull herself out of bed in the morning, which was unusual because all her life she had bounced out of bed, ready and eager to greet a new day. Occasionally she had queasy spells. She was so tired when night came, she went to her room right after supper. Charles mentioned several times that she looked peaked and she often caught her mother-in-law watching her intently.

Mrs. Horne cooked up a brew of herbs that she said would help if Sally Day's only trouble was thin blood. The bitter brew made Sally Day so sick she couldn't keep it down. Right then and there Mrs. Horne made the decision. "Charles, I want you to take Sarah to see Dr. Strong this very day."

Charles left Sally Day at the doctor's door and waited for her in the buggy. Dr. Strong was stout, red faced and cheerful like his brother who kept the Jericho store. He was also an elder of the church, and town talk said he was the one who had held up the vote on the minister's dismissal.

He took Sally Day's cloak and put her in a chair and began to ask questions. The eyes behind his steel-rimmed glasses were sharp. Finally he reached over and patted her hand and asked, "Sally Day, haven't you guessed what's happened to you?"

"No," she said.

"Then I've got a very wonderful piece of news for you," he said happily. "You're going to have a baby."

Chapter Fifteen

S HE WAS CRYING with shock and happiness when Dr. Strong fetched Charles in to tell him. He blurted out, stunned, "She can't be having a baby, she's only seventeen!"

"That would be news to Mother Nature," Dr. Strong chuckled. "Maybe she can't be, but she is."

Charles seemed too dazed to know what he was doing, and Dr. Strong accompanied them to the buggy and tucked the buffalo robe around Sally Day. "Take care of this little girl," he advised, "but don't treat her like a china doll. She's a healthy young lady and there's no reason she shouldn't have a perfect and healthy baby."

"Does she need any medicine?" Charles asked. "My mother thought she ought to have a tonic."

"She doesn't need any medicine, only good food and plenty of sleep and a normal amount of work. And happy thoughts," Dr. Strong added. "But don't tell me Elizabeth Horne didn't guess the truth for I know she did."

Charles called "Giddap" to Ebenezer. Suddenly such happiness as Sally Day had never seen flamed in her husband's face. He stood up in the buggy and let out a yell of pure joy. Everybody on Main Street turned and stared.

Sally Day pulled him down in the seat to make him behave. Was this her quiet, reserved husband?

She herself was so happy and upset and frightened all at the same time, she couldn't sort out how she really felt. During the drive home they agreed to keep the momentous fact to themselves, at least for awhile. "Just until I get a little used to the idea," Sally Day explained.

When they drove into the barnyard and Charles helped her down, she noticed that the kitchen curtain twitched aside. Mrs. Horne glanced up from her cooking as they enntered. The two women looked at each other for a long moment, then Sally Day rushed into her mother-in-law's arms.

Mrs. Horne smoothed her hair with a rough palm. "There, there, Sarah," she whispered. "It's as I guessed, isn't it?"

"Mrs. Horne, are you pleased?" Sally Day asked.

"As pleased as your own mother will be and that's saying a lot," the older woman assured her. "And surely now the time's come for you to stop calling me 'Mrs.' We'll get pretty well acquainted, dear, before we're through this. I'll take it kindly if you'll call me 'Mother.'"

Charles changed into his work clothes and joined his father in the woodlot on the hill. All day Sally Day heard the ring of their axes as they worked together up there. Was Charles telling his father the news? Now that her mother-in-law had guessed, Ezra Horne would have to know, too. Sally Day realized, We didn't manage to keep it a secret very long.

She spent part of that afternoon in her room alone. She was so nervous she felt as though she could fly, and hoped that would go away once she got used to what was happening to her. She studied her face in the mirror and marveled that she still looked like the Sally Day she was used to meeting in the glass.

The men came in at dusk. Mr. Horne's heavy feet dragged. As usual he washed at the slate sink, then took his place at the table to be waited on. No, Charles had said nothing, that was clear.

After supper a fellow elder of the church came to call, but Mr. Horne took him out to the barn so they could talk undisturbed. The man left early. The rest of the family was still gathered in the kitchen when its head came in.

He stood rubbing his hands together over the hot stove. Nobody asked him why his friend had come or what they had discussed, and he had to bring up the subject himself. He addressed Charles directly, "I heard tonight there's been plotting in my own house, behind my back," he said. "Chester Jackson tells me you met with some other young fellers to figure ways and means of keeping the minister here. It won't be a bit of use no matter how many meetings you hold. The votes are against him, despite what Doc Strong and his brother do."

If Sally Day hadn't been listening, how would Charles have answered? She saw how hard it was for him to go against the older man, because the habit of obedience was so strong. He gave her a glance and muttered, "It's wrong and there's no reason to it. The Reverend has done a fine job. He's got the young people coming to the church and enjoying it—"

"He's introduced enough new fangled notions to last any church a lifetime," Mr. Horne interrupted. "But the candles and that claptrap aren't so important. The fact is that he's said right out, plain as day, there isn't any hell. That's the big danger. You go cutting hell out of religion and there's not much left. No, he's got to go back to divinity school and learn his lessons over."

Sally Day couldn't keep silent. Why should she? Her position in this house had changed radically and she knew it. She had done quite solemn thinking, up in her bedroom that afternoon. This family she had married into had a future now, and she was the one who was giving it to them. Her child was their link with the future and all the generations to come.

She had seen this with sudden clarity and it wiped out her fear of Mr. Horne's annoyance. "I've listened carefully to Mr. Crawford's sermons because he talks good sense," she said. "He never said there wasn't a hell, he only said most people find theirs right here on earth, and their heaven, too, if they've got the wits to look for it. Why, everybody knows that most of that talk about fire and brimstone in the hot place is just to scare children with!"

"There!" Mr. Horne exclaimed triumphantly. "If anybody needed proof of what dangerous notions young Crawford has sown, here it is right in my own house."

"It's time we went to bed," Mrs. Horne put in then.

Sally Day noticed how pale she was. The clue to all the trouble in this house was the fact that Ezra Horne's own wife acted as though she was afraid of him. That was a terrible thing in any home, to have the mistress afraid of the master. Sally Day simply couldn't bear it, for she had grown up in a home where nobody was afraid of anybody. Besides, a very real affection had been growing slowly during the last few weeks, between her and her mother-in-law.

Sally Day began sorting out in her mind the things she longed to say, the harsh truths, the words that would really make Ezra Horne stop and think. She didn't get her chance though, for she waited too long.

"It doesn't matter what the young folks do, not the way our church is set up," Mr. Horne said. "Votes are what matter. Chester Jackson claims we've got the votes that will insure a new minister coming to Jericho."

He set his boots down with a thump, to keep warm by the stove until morning, and started for the stairs. "Mr. Horne," his wife said, "I think Sarah has something she wants to tell you."

He turned. "Well?"

Sally Day looked him straight in the eye and said, "No, there's a mistake. There isn't a thing in the world I want to tell you, Mr. Horne." She slipped by him and darted up the stairs.

Charles got up before dawn as usual the next morning, but when she stirred he tucked the quilts tightly around her and ordered, "You stay and sleep. Ma told me you're to get some extra rest in the mornings."

She awoke again hours later to pale daylight and a howling world outside. A blizzard had struck during the early hours. High winds drove the whirling snow against the window and the room was like an icehouse. She dressed rapidly so she wouldn't turn into an icicle and hurried downstairs.

Mrs. Horne gave her light, easy tasks. It was while Sally Day was holding a skein of yarn for her that Mrs. Horne brought up the unpleasantness of the previous evening. "You hadn't ought to rile Mr. Horne," she said. "You shouldn't mind too much what he says. His bark is worse than his bite."

Sally Day thought, I doubt that, but kept still.

"I told him about the baby. It isn't right to keep from him what the rest of us know."

"And what did he say?"

"I don't recollect that he said anything."

He still said nothing when he came in for dinner. Actually his eyes seemed to avoid Sally Day. She thought grimly, All right, old man, you keep your silence and I'll keep mine.

The snow and gale-force winds continued all day with no letup. Sally Day was restless, moving from window to window. A wall of white had surrounded the farm. Snow swirled across the fields, piling against the outbuildings. She watched her husband doggedly reshoveling the paths he had made earlier. The shocks of corn still left in the cornfield beyond the barn took on the weird look of white soldiers carrying heavy white packs. She remembered how excited and happy she had been over the first December snowstorm and mused, I must have been out of my mind to think there was anything pretty about snow.

There was little conversation at supper. Mrs. Horne asked after the animals. Charles confided to Sally Day that he had made a special corner for Duke in a wooden box lined with a horse blanket. He knew that she worried about her friend.

There was no use mentioning it, but Sally Day longed for the dog's company, longed to have him in the house. Maybe Duke couldn't talk but there was a lot of comfort in his kind of silence, in a home where human silence seemed louder than words.

She expected to wake the next morning to sunshine and a crystal world but the storm was still whirling over the land. There was no mention of choir practice, and obviously she and Charles would have to miss it. Perhaps it wouldn't be held anyway: Charles told her that Jericho was probably snowbound, the roads clogged, the town isolated from the rest of the state. He figured that four feet of snow had fallen but it was hard to tell because it had drifted so. Sally Day that morning had discovered a drift that had climbed fiftteen feeet to her bedroom window.

"How long will it be before we get out?" she asked.

"Maybe a week."

"It can't be. I'll go out of my mind if I don't get out of the house in a whole week!"

"No, you won't go out of your mind, Sally Day."

It was all he and his father could do just to keep the farm going, bringing in armfuls of wood for the kitchen range, filling the water buckets, carrying slops and grain for the hens and pigs, hauling down hay from the loft for the cows and horses and sheep. Sally Day realized that living on a farm in winter was sometimes just a grim battle to survive.

Something happened to her during those snowbound days. The others worked too hard to pay much attention to her, and she had too much time for thinking. A lot of new questions began buzzing inside her head. Did she really want to be a farmer's wife? Was she in tune with this kind of a life and would she ever be? Did the Hornes endure this harsh existence because they actually liked it, or because they were trapped in it?

She and Charles were never alone except at night. During the day everyone stayed as close as possible to the kitchen stove. Only when they huddled in their featherbed could they talk together. Usually Charles was so dog tired he fell asleep the minute his head hit the pillow. Finally, on the third night of the storm, Sally Day began to question him.

She did it carefully, for she had finally learned that you

didn't blurt out everything to a husband no matter how much you loved him. "Charles," she said, "I suppose you won't have to work quite so hard when we're in our own home on our own farm."

"I don't know about that, but I don't mind hard work," he said.

"It couldn't be as hard because we'll have to start out small, with only a few cows and a few acres cleared."

"I'll still help Pa on his land. That's the way we planned it. He and I will go shares."

"How early can we start building our house? In May? April, maybe?"

"Sally Day, did I ever say positively that we'd build this spring?"

"Of course you did, Charles!"

"I doubt I did, because I wasn't that sure myself."

"What do you mean?"

"What I said was that I hoped to build, and I still hope to. But Pa and I had hard luck with our cash crop last summer, so we're a little short of money now."

"What do you mean?"

"Our money crop is broad leaf tobacco," he explained. "Just about the time we were ready to cut and hang it, a hailstorm struck and shredded half of it. That was a total loss. The good half didn't bring the price Pa had hoped for, either."

"Charles, how could you have failed to tell me an important thing like that?" she cried.

"Shhh," he warned her. Then he said slowly, "It's my own fault, but up to now I fear I've treated you like a child instead of a wife. That's how I thought of you, Sally Day, as a child wife. I didn't tell you about the tobacco because I didn't want you to give up your pretty dream of a little house of your own. I'm not saying that it's impossible, for I may yet see my way clear to start building. That depends on Pa, whether he'll loan us the money."

"Why do we have to ask him? Why can't we borrow from a bank?"

"The Hornes don't go into debt to banks."

She started to say that it seemed worse to her to be dependant on Ezra Horne's goodwill. "Don't talk against my father to me, please don't," he pleaded. "Most of the time I feel as though I'm being ground between two millstones."

"I'm sorry about that," she said softly.

On the fourth day the storm stopped, the wind died and the sun turned the landscape to a blinding, glittering white. That afternoon a team of heavy work horses from town floundered through the drifts, dragging the huge wooden roller that made the road passable. On the following day Charles managed to get to Jericho, to purchase the basic supplies his mother needed.

He was pleased to be able to bring a letter home to Sally Day. He found her in the buttery, so they were alone. He hung about while she opened it, curious because he had noticed that it wasn't from Maryland.

"It's from Tillman," she said, to satisfy his curiosity. She noted that this information quenched the pleased look on his face. "Here, I'll read it.

" 'Dear little cousin, this will surprise you for you probably didn't know I could write! Yes, here I am at Harvard, in Boston, right in the heart of Yankeeland. My mother and my sisters believe I've turned traitor and gone over to the enemy, but Judge Sayres in Elkton advised me to come here to study law. Harvard also is supposed to teach me to be a scholar and a gentleman but what could a Southerner learn from the Northerners about that?

" 'Your devoted family is anxious about you and your parents were overjoyed when I suggested I might call on you and learn first hand how you are prospering as a married woman. I trust this will not go against your husband's wishes. Since the post office is irregular I shall not try to warn you of my coming but shall simply appear one day soon in Jericho. My visit will be brief, as I cannot take much time away from my studies. Mama sold her matched sapphires in order to give me a Yankee education so I must make the most of it.' "

By now Sally Day wished with all her heart she had read the letter first, so she could give Charles the gist of it. Tillman's flip way of talking might bother someone who didn't know him well. She had nothing to hide from her husband though, did she? No, she decided. She read the ending, "With cousinly love, from your devoted Tillman."

It was on the tip of Sally Day's tongue to say, "Oh, dear, it's too bad but he mustn't come."

Charles said it first, "It's absolutely impossible for him to come here."

His tone made Sally Day switch right around. "Why?" she demanded.

"Because we don't entertain company here," Charles said flatly.

"He's not company, he's my very own first cousin, and there's nothing we can do about it because he can't let us know when to expect him," Sally Day pointed out. "Unless you put your foot down, Charles, and make me turn away my own blood kin at the door, then we'll have to let him come."

Charles saw that he had been put in the wrong and re-luctantly agreed.

Sally Day told her mother-in-law next of the threatened visit. Mrs. Horne looked stunned at the very idea, but agreed, too, there seemed no way to avoid it. Sally Day promised it would be a short one, that Tillman would stay only a night or two. Charles talked to his father in private. Mr. Horne was so paralysed by the notion of a stranger staying in his house, the fact that the guest had been a Con-federate soldier didn't anger him as much as Sally Day ex-pected.

By turns she dreaded and longed for her cousin's coming, but she didn't have many days to wait. The snow from the big blizzard still covered the country when one evening at early dusk an unfamiliar rig came up the lane and Tillman alighted.

Sally Day rushed to the door and her cousin caught her in his arms and swung her off the ground. Overjoyed to see each other, they entered the kitchen laughing, where the three Hornes at the table turned grim faces towards them. Sally Day felt a giggle like a bubble rising inside her, for she noticed that her own dear husband's face was the grimmest of the three.

She had forgotten how gay, how gallant her blond, merry cousin could be. He sat down at the table and turned on all his charm. He treated Mrs. Horne like a grande dame, acted frankly and openly friendly to Charles, deferred to Mr. Horne respectfully. Mr. Horne had a hard time lifting his own eyes higher than Tillman's ruffled, silk shirt. There was no getting around it, in his close-fitting fawn suit, Tillman did look like a dandy.

He addressed the master of the house directly. "I reckon

it's real hard for you to let a Secesh into your house, Mr. Horne," he said. "I can appreciate that, sir. My little cousin's family is longing for first-hand news of her, and that's my only excuse for breaking in on you this way."

Actually it was Tillman's ignorance that saved him. He couldn't possibly understand what it meant to the Hornes to have a former enemy eating at their table.

Sally Day guessed that she might eventually pay for the effrontery of this visit, so she decided to enjoy it while it lasted. Tillman stayed the next day and a second night. A perfect guest, he trimmed his sails to the winds that blew around him. He talked about cooking with Mrs. Horne, visited the barn and discussed livestock and crops with the men. He never tried to catch Sally Day alone for a bit of cousinly gossip.

Nobody invited him to prolong his visit, but he didn't seem to notice. "I hired my rig from a stable in Norwich to drive up here, and I can't waste my mother's money by keeping it any longer," he explained.

Sally Day put his mind at rest in case he wondered about the brooch he had given her. She wore her blue delaine and pinned it to hold the lace collar. Tillman's eyes lit up when he saw it, and didn't notice that Mr. Horne glowered. He had no way of knowing that Sally's wearing the large, expensive brooch was like waving a red rag at a bull.

Everybody went outside to see him off, although Sally Day suspected that the Horne men did it to speed him on his journey. Tillman kissed her in a fervent way that was still cousinly and respectful, said, "I'll write your folks I found you happy and in blooming health, little Sally Day," and was gone with a gay wave of his hand.

It was with real gratitude that she thanked the Hornes for their courtesy to her guest. She had to give them credit, they had their own kind of good manners. None of them mentioned they thought Tillman was a fop and a dandy, or that he had shown incredible nerve to come visiting in a Yankee home. No, after Tillman's rig clattered out of the yard they simply pretended that the visit had never happened. They never mentioned it or him again.

They couldn't change one fact, though. For two days there had been gaiety in the house. Maybe they didn't share in it but it had been there. For a few hours Tillman had pushed away the heavy dullness that hung over the farm like a pall, and Sally Day was grateful.

Chapter Sixteen

AFTERWARDS, TILLMAN'S SHORT visit seemed to be a brighter event than it actually was. The winter was dragging on interminably and Sally Day began to believe it would never end. With each passing day the house seemed more like a jail. Being house-bound was making her so nervous she was ready to fly.

She was beginning to think that Charles was quite a dull sort. He didn't care whether he went anywhere or not, and when a plan was suggested to him his first reaction was "No."

"Let's go and call on the Crawfords," she suggested once.

"No," Charles said. "The minister pays calls but people don't pay calls on him."

"But they'd love to have us! Charlotte Crawford said the other day when I saw her in the store that she wished you and I would drop in for a cup of coffee."

Charles said gloomily, "I'm sorry, Sally Day, but I don't have the time right now for any socializing."

"Maybe when spring comes you'll have even less time, and when summer comes you won't have any time at all!"

Then out of the blue a nice thing happened. Sally Day guessed that the other women of Jericho were just as desperate as she was to get out of their houses. After church one Sunday, when people were standing around outside in the yard enjoying the weekly exchange of news, Jane Cope's mother happened to mention that she had two quilts ready to put together. Jane suggested, "Mother, let's have a quilting party."

"Why, that might be a nice idea," her mother agreed, and right there she invited the Horne ladies and some others for an evening party during the following week.

Sally Day bubbled all the way home in the sleigh. Although Mrs. Horne had been invited, too, she seemed to take it for granted she wasn't going. When Sally Day realized this she exclaimed "Of course you're going, Mother!" She was amused to see how Mr. Horne's back stiffened at this familiarity.

She nagged all the next day her mother-in-law. Finally Mrs. Horne admitted, "I haven't got a dress to wear in the evening."

"You have, too!" Sally Day declared. "You look truly elegant in your Sunday black, and if you'll just dress it up with my gold brooch you'll be the best-dressed woman there."

Mr. Horne's silence indicated he disapproved of such frivolity. When the two ladies came down dressed for the Copes' party, and he saw the brooch pinned to the lace collar of his wife's dress, he actually snorted.

Her eyes begged him not to be annoyed. Sally Day noticed this and turned hot with sudden anger. No woman ought to have to treat any man that way. Fearful that Mrs. Horne would give in and stay home, or else take off the offending pin, Sally Day seized her arm and hurried her out to the sleigh.

Charles was to drive them to town and hang around until ten, when he would pick them up and bring them home. The Cope house was a blaze of lights when Ebenezer trotted along Main Street. "They don't care how they waste oil," Charles commented.

Sally Day was so excited at the prospect of a party she was practically jumping out of her skin. Charles saw then the happiness in her face, and gave her hand a squeeze as he handed her down. "Don't you get all tired out," he said.

The ladies called out greetings when the two entered. "I'm so pleased you talked Elizabeth Horne into coming," Mrs. Cope whispered to Sally Day as she took their wraps. "She hasn't had very many good times in her life."

About twenty had gathered, older women and girls Jane's and Sally Day's age. Two quilting frames had been set up, one in the parlor and the other in Mr. Cope's law library across the hall. He was the town lawyer, and used his house as his office. The doors were open between the rooms so that the ladies could visit back and forth.

Sally Day chose to sew with her mother-in-law on a quilt made in the pine tree pattern. Mrs. Cope had laid out an intricate design of stitching.

At first Sally Day was careless about her stitches. It was hard work putting the needle through the patchwork top, then through the cotton batting filling, and the muslin backing. She chattered like a magpie, trying to draw her mother-in-law into the conversation. Then she realized that her stitches were getting too big and recalled the teaching she had received from Miss Trimble, the dressmaker at home. She worked in tiny stitches, and noticed that Mrs. Horne looked relieved that she knew how to quilt properly.

"Where's Charlotte Crawford?" she asked. "I didn't see

her when we came in. Is she in the other room?"

"She isn't coming," someone said.

"Why ever not?"

Mrs. Strong, the doctor's wife, who was quilting across from the Horne ladies, said reluctantly, "Mrs. Crawford just learned today that her husband will probably be leaving Jericho, and I guess she was too upset to come out tonight."

That put a damper on the gaiety. Sally Day realized that the other ladies knew that Ezra Horne was one of the prime movers against the minister, and took it for granted Mrs. Horne would agree with him. She said loudly so all would hear, "That's too bad. My mother and I feel badly that the town may lose such nice folks as the Crawfords."

Some color appeared in Mrs. Horne's pale cheeks, hearing herself called "Mother." However she agreed, "Yes, the town will miss them."

Then the others relaxed, knowing how the Horne women stood in the matter. Mrs. Strong went on, "The minister and my husband often work together, Mr. Strong being a doctor. Not very long ago something happened and I wish the whole town knew of it. Strangers, a family named Eaton, moved into a house down on the flats. My husband got a call to go there because Mr. Eaton had fallen out of his haymow and had broken his arm. He found they were quite nice folks, poor but clean. The wife was real upset that she couldn't pay the doctor for making the calls.

"Then it came out she'd had a letter that day from her son in Chicago. It seems as if in this world troubles never come singly, and her son had written he was in a hospital in Chicago and feared he had consumption. Mrs. Eaton gathered from what he said that he didn't expect to live and the letter was goodbye.

"She was in a terrible state, as you can imagine. This was her only son who had gone west to seek his fortune. The doctor happened to mention all this to Mr. Crawford, when they met later that day.

"When he went out the next time to look at Mr. Eaton's arm and take him some food, my husband found Mr. Eaton alone. His wife had gone to Chicago. The minister had paid her train fare. It cost over forty dollars, so that meant Mr. Crawford had given her just about what the church pays him for a whole month's wages."

There was a silence. Someone asked, "Did the son die?"

"No," Mrs. Strong said. "It turned out he had pneumonia instead, and his mother nursed him and brought him home. I can tell you, that family sees Mr. Crawford as a saint."

All the ladies' heads were bent over their quilting but Sally Day saw they were thinking hard. Jane Cope burst out with what was on all their minds. "We've got to stop their leaving! But how can we do it if the elders vote against Mr. Crawford?"

Mrs. Anderson cleared her throat and sounded embarrassed but determined. "As you probably all know, my husband's one of the elders who believes we need a change. He and I are at swords' points over it, I admit. Now, I've come up with an idea. All the elders except the Strongs are acting like sheep in the matter. Please excuse me for saying so, since some of your husbands are numbered among them. I thought we women might write to the District Superintendent and give him our views, stating that we like the Crawfords, telling some of the fine things the minister has done. If we all sign the letter and get other women who aren't here tonight to sign, and also some of the men who are sitting on the fence in the matter, it might turn the trick."

A babble of talk broke out then. Mrs. Anderson and Mrs. Strong were sent away from the quilting into another room to write the letter. It was read and corrected and written again, and then each lady signed it.

It gave Sally Day a great feeling of happiness to sign under her mother-in-law's "Mrs. Ezra Horne" her own "Mrs. Charles Horne." Did the others know how much courage it required of Elizabeth Horne to put her name to such a paper?

The evening was drawing on. The quilting wasn't finished, but the men would come at ten to collect their ladies. The guests were called into the dining room where a bountiful collation was spread, of tea and cakes and tarts. All the ladies made a real fuss over Elizabeth Horne and made sure her plate was filled with good things. Sally Day realized then that they were well aware of her courage in going against her husband.

Buggies were lined up in the street but none of the menfolk had the courage to come inside to get warm because the house was filled with women. Sally Day and Mrs. Horne emerged into the crisp night.

"Did you have a good time?" Charles asked, as Ebenezer started home.

"Yes," Sally Day said, and added, "we had a good time and we put a spoke in your father's wheel."

"What do you mean?"

Sally Day told him. "Such a letter might work, for the District Superintendent wouldn't dare ignore it," Charles said slowly. "Ma, did you sign?"

"Yes, son, I did."

Charles made no comment, he only groaned.

When Ezra Horne learned what had been done, not from them but in a roundabout way from the other elders, he laid down the law to the whole household. He charged his wife with disloyalty. She took it meekly and made no reply. She continued to pay for her intransigeance, for her husband's silence was a constant reproach.

She wasn't sorry though. Sally Day knew that beyond any doubt, for there was a sparkle in the older woman's eyes Sally Day had never seen in them before.

Gradually, Mr. Horne changed. He didn't become suddenly affable, but Sally Day caught him watching his wife when he thought no one was looking. He seemed to be trying to figure out what was going on in her mind. He acted unsure of himself. Just the threat of his displeasure had once been his best weapon. Now it seemed to be losing its force.

The letter worked. As chairman of the Board of Elders, Mr. Horne received a communication from the District Superintendent asking that the final vote be delayed until he could come to Jericho to discuss the matter. The tide turned, and several of the elders sheepishly informed their chairman that they had changed their minds.

Ezra Horne didn't give in easily. He proceeded to try to punish both his family and the minister by refusing to go to church as long as Mr. Crawford occupied the pulpit. This was no punishment at all, as far as Sally Day was concerned. She looked forward all week to church without her father-in-law's heavy company.

Mrs. Cope gave another party so that the ladies could finish the work they had started. This time Mrs. Horne didn't go because her husband acted so ornery when he heard about it. Sally Day guessed he feared the ladies might get involved in some new, iniquitous project at a gay and worldly event like a quilting party. She was sorry her mother-in-law gave in but didn't blame her, for Sally Day was learning that marriage was a matter of give and take. Mr. Horne had suffered a defeat, so his wife was trying to make it up to him by giving in meekly.

Well, he wasn't Sally Day's husband and she could very well bear up under his disapproval and she went. This time Charlotte Crawford came, and the two rushed into each other's arms. There was no weighty talk this time, just light-hearted chatter over the quilting frames. Sally Day couldn't keep her own momentous news to herself any longer, and confided to Charlotte, who was sewing next to her, that she was expecting. That news soon flew around the quilting frames like wildfire and all her friends gathered around Sally Day to kiss and congratulate her.

During the next few weeks, Sally Day decided there was nothing at all to the business of having a baby. She no longer felt any queasiness or nausea, she actually felt better and stronger than she ever had in her life. She was filled with energy, and it seemed to her that if spring didn't come soon she would burst out of her prison, the walls that kept her housebound.

A thaw came late in February, and the thermometer rose to sixty. The snow turned to dirty slush and ran off in sudden brooks. The air had an exciting smell of fresh, moist earth. Sally Day sat on the kitchen doorstep with no cloak or shawl about her, enjoying the sun.

Her mother-in-law found her there and tried to put her shawl around her. Sally Day demanded, "What comes out first?"

"What do you mean?"

"I mean flowers."

"Oh. Not flowers, child. Skunk cabbage comes first, and after that the pussy willows, but it's probably too early for them."

Sally Day jumped up. "Let's go and see."

Mrs. Horne laughed nervously, not believing she was serious. "Child, we can't just up and go for a walk in the midst of a working day."

"Yes, we can. There's no law in the United States or Connecticut or even Jericho that says a woman can't drop her work for an hour and look for skunk cabbage." Sally Day took Mrs. Horne's shawl from its hook and wrapped it around her and dragged her along.

The men were mending stone walls in the west forty, each working along his own side of the wall putting back the rocks which had fallen during the winter. Charles had taken off his shirt.

He saw Sally Day and waved, but his father didn't look around. Mrs. Horne sort of scurried along the sunken road. When she acted this way, as though she feared her husband's disapproval, Sally Day inevitably got angry. She didn't say anything for she didn't want to spoil their walk, but she thought to herself, I'll manage my life better. No matter what happens I won't let myself be afraid of any man.

They reached the swamp, but here the snow was too high for Sally Day to wade through in her gaiters. Mrs. Horne shyly said that they might find pussy willows along the road, further on. "So this isn't the first time you've sneaked off to look for them!" Sally Day cried triumphantly.

Her mother-in-law blushed. "I went a few times, when I was young like you."

Sure enough they found the willows, but the soft gray

kittens hadn't started to develop. "We'll pick them anyway and put them in water, and maybe we'll get pussies on them," Sally Day said. She borrowed the knife which Mrs. Horne carried with her keys, on a chain around her waist.

Sally Day cut a bunch, then handed back the knife. "I can hardly wait until I get a key chain of my own," she said. "Oh, it must be lovely to have your own house and your keys!"

"Perhaps you will next year, if we have a good summer and the tobacco does well," Mrs. Horne assured her.

Sally Day had her mouth open to say that a year was too long, that she would never survive a full year of feeling like a guest in Mr. Horne's house. She shut her mouth with a snap. There were a lot of things she longed to confide to her mother-in-law, but the time was not ripe. She had to make up her own mind, and determine her own true feelings on some important matters, before she confided in anyone, even in Charles.

Clouds had moved in from the west, growing heavier as they covered the sky. The sun faded and the air was chilly. The women turned homeward.

A rusty, black buggy was standing in the yard, and a gaunt and ancient horse nodded, its head bent low. The man hunched up on the doorstone looked even older than his equipment. "Excuse me sitting at your door, Mis' Horne," he said ingratiatingly. "I was just too plumb tired to move."

"Why, it's the peddler," Mrs. Horne exclaimed. "Johnnie, isn't that your name?"

" 'Johnnie,' that's right, ma'am. I was here two years ago and you bought some things from me. Did the mail bring them all right?"

"Yes, they came. What are you doing on the roads this

time of year?"

"I got caught with too little money to see me through the winter, so I came out of hibernation early," he said with a grin. "This your daughter, Mis' Horne? A lady in town told me your son married. Mighty pretty girl he got!"

"Are you hungry?" Mrs. Horne asked.

"Ma'am, I'm always hungry. Now I'm hungry and cold, too." He wrapped the rags of his tattered coat about him.

Mrs. Horne glanced nervously over the fields where her husband was working, then said, "You can come in, Johnnie."

Sally Day put the soup kettle on to heat and set bread and butter and preserves in front of him. Each time he caught her glance he smiled a toothless smile, but never stopped talking while he ate.

He ate so much Sally Day began to think his stomach must be a bottomless pit, but at last he pushed his chair back and admitted he was full. Then he went to his wagon to fetch his samples.

He spread them out on the table. Sally Day hung over them, fascinated, for she had never seen anything like them. He carried the usual line of thread, needles, ribbons, and besides these he showed miniatures of bulkier objects he hoped to sell. As he traveled the country he showed his miniatures and the country wives chose what they wanted. The real articles came later by mail.

He held up a cunningly made, tiny copper kettle. "Wouldn't a pretty girl like you appreciate a new, shiny kettle?" he wheedled.

Sally Day laughed. "I don't need a kettle for I live in Mrs. Horne's house and she's already got one. But I'd love to have this toy one."

"That I can't sell, my dear, for I need it to show."

Mrs. Horne ordered a new iron spider for frying. Sally Day chose a length of red velvet ribbon for her hair and a packet of needles.

The men came in just as they finished making their selections. The peddler also carried small models of tools, and from these Mr. Horne purchased a hoe, a scythe and a hammer. He grumbled that Johnnie's prices were higher than he would pay at the store in Jericho, but Johnnie pointed out that his quality was better.

Sally Day helped him put his toylike samples back in their cases. "Now, if you'll let me borrow a corner of your barn for the night for me and my horse, I won't bother you further and we'll be gone in the morning," Johnnie said.

Sally Day forgot it wasn't her place to offer hospitality. "We've got an empty guest room," she suggested.

Mr. Horne countermanded that. "Charles, take him out and show him where he can bed down."

Sally Day offered no argument. If this was my real home in Maryland, though, she thought rebelliously, even a ragged peddler would be given a bed in the house and a place at the family table.

After Charles had gone with Johnnie she did ask Mrs. Horne quietly why he couldn't at least sleep on the kitchen floor. Mr. Horne overheard and answered, "Because he's probably got fleas, and worse than that he probably carries bedbugs in his rags."

Charles came back and they sat down. "Did you bring the lantern in with you?" his father asked. Charles nodded.

"I do think we could let him have a light," Sally Day protested.

"We can't because he'd probably set the barn on fire,"

Mr. Horne said. "Did you lock him in, Charles?"

"No."

"Go and do it then."

"But why?" Sally Day cried. "You treat him like a prisoner instead of a guest!"

"I'll tell you why, young lady," Mr. Horne scowled, raising his eyebrows at her. "Once we did give a peddler the use of our barn, and the next morning we found him gone and along with him everything that wasn't nailed down!"

"It still seems like an awful way to treat a guest," Sally Day murmured, wishing to drop the argument but unable to.

"I suppose where you come from you lay out the best china and put fresh linen sheets on the bed for the likes of him?"

"No, but we'd give him blankets, and we wouldn't lock him in the barn, and he'd certainly eat at the table with us. That's the Christian way."

"So now you're telling me my Christian duty! Let me tell you, young lady—"

She didn't give Mr. Horne a chance to tell her. She ran to her room and burrowed under the bedclothes.

Chapter Seventeen

A T DAWN THE next morning Johnnie was ready to set out on his journey. Charles carried a hot breakfast out to him and he ate sitting in the sun, in the wide doorway of the barn.

His rattly buggy lurched down the lane. "Poor soul," Mrs. Horne said, watching him from the kitchen window.

"I don't feel sorry for him," Sally Day told her.

"Why ever not? You're so tender-hearted you'd bring the chickens and pigs into the house if we let you," Charles said. They hadn't heard him come in.

"He can go where he wishes," Sally Day said in a low voice.

"What do you mean, Sarah?" Mrs. Horne asked.

"I mean he's free. He could go to the city, he could go to the west, he could go south where it's warm." Sally Day knew she had said too much, and abruptly left the room.

"I'm a mite worried about her," she heard Mrs. Horne say, and heard Charles's admission, "So am I."

For quite a long time, in fact ever since the trouble over the minister, an idea had been bumbling around in Sally Day's mind. This morning, Johnnie's departure clarified it. She had spoken the truth when she said she wasn't sorry for the old peddler. What she had actually felt was sharp envy.

Their bedroom was cold as "Greenland's icy mountains," but she wanted to be alone. She got into bed with all her clothes on, drew up the down quilt, and huddled over her writing portfolio. "Dear Papa," she began. She went on to tell him that she was feeling fine and that all was well with her. Her family already knew about the baby; she had written them that joyful news when she first learned of it.

She carefully balanced the inkwell on the bedside table because it would be a tragedy if she spilled ink on the bed, and chewed the end of her quill pen. She wanted to strike exactly the right, casual note. "Papa," she wrote, "I've had a lot of time to think about things this winter, and observe and study, and I've begun to wonder if Charles and I wouldn't be happier if we lived somewhere else. Of course what I mean by 'somewhere else' is Maryland.

"Mama wrote me that you had to hire an extra hand to work at the store after I went away, because she's too busy at home to help out. Now I ask myself if it wouldn't be a real help to you if we moved down to Chesapeake City and Charles worked with you at the Emporium.

"You know me, Papa, and you know I'm selfish and that I'm not thinking of your welfare and how nice it would be for you to have Charles's help. No, as usual I'm thinking of my own good.

"We wouldn't move in to live with you. We would rent a couple of rooms in town, and start building a little house near Chesapeake City."

Sally Day had meant to make this letter a reasonable kind of business proposition, but now the tears were falling. All the pentup loneliness and homesickness and tension of the long, long winter were welling up inside her. "I don't rightly

see how I can stand it any longer," she wrote. "I just can't
live in a house where people are so silent and afraid to be
happy. I adore my husband and I think that he'd be a new
person if he could get away from here."

She carefully dried her face. The men were still mending walls, and Mrs. Horne had set herself a big stint of wool
to card this morning, so there was little danger of anyone
walking in and finding Sally Day dissolved in tears. But
she was trying to get hold of her dignity. She wrote, "I ought
to do this letter over and leave that last part out, for I owe
the Hornes loyalty. You and Mama were right to teach me
that was my duty. Will you think this over as a business proposition, and write me how you feel? Your loving daughter."

This problem of duty was a knotty one, she thought so-
berly, as she sealed the letter. It was certainly disloyal to her
husband to write such a letter to her father. But that was
the way it had to be done. There was no point at all in
talking to Charles now about moving to Maryland. That
would only start an argument that would be pointless if she
didn't have her father's word he needed Charles at the store
and wanted them to come.

She felt so guilty about going behind Charles's back she
went out of her way, during the next few days, to be meek,
to try to keep out of trouble. Charles took her letter to
town to mail. When she asked to go along, too, he pointed
out that the frozen ruts would throw the buggy about and
make the drive dangerous for her. She assured him mildly,
"I'll do just as you say."

She figured it might be ten days before she received her
answer. She guessed she'd be able to act like a proper wife
and daughter-in-law that long.

Then one day she overhead the elder Hornes talking.

Mr. Horne came into the kitchen, and apparently his wife forgot that Sally Day was tidying the dish shelves in the buttery. "Is Sarah all right?" Mr. Horne asked.

"I suppose so," his wife told him, "though I do worry about her, for she's a fragile little thing."

"Seems to me I haven't heard the sound of her voice for days." Mr. Horne uttered his harsh laugh. "Maybe I was beginning to get used to her spitting at me. It does seem like Charles was asking trouble for himself when he went out of the state to choose a bride."

"He loves her, that's clear," Mrs. Horne said.

"Yes, and she's a pretty mite, and fair clever with her hands. Still, handsome is as handsome does and I misdoubt she'll ever be able to manage the heavy work of running a farm."

Sally Day was astonished, for she had no idea that the couple ever talked together this way, like real married folks. It had also given her quite a turn to hear her father-in-law admit she was a "pretty mite."

Second thought told her, however, he would have to admit considerably more than that before she and he would get along well. He would have to admit, for instance, that although she was a woman she was entitled to respect. He would also have to get over the notion that he could keep Charles as an unpaid hired man on the home farm.

She ticked off seven days, waiting for the answer to her letter. The waiting was hard, but deceiving Charles was harder. She felt twitchy with nervousness.

On an afternoon when the sun lay warm on the land, she decided, I'll go and look for that skunk cabbage again. The snow was gone except for pockets along walls and fences, but there were no signs of green yet. Nostalgia shot through her like a sharp pain as she realized that at home the forsythia was beginning to bloom, showering its gold in all the yards in town.

"Do you need me for an hour, ma'am?" she asked Mrs. Horne.

"No, child. Go and take a little walk, it'll do you good."

Sally Day didn't need to whistle for Duke because he was lurking just inside the barn door, hoping she would emerge. They started out. Then Sally Day turned back. Why should the older woman stay house bound on this spring-smelling day?

Mrs. Horne was in the carding room, working on the awful, dusty wool. "Mother, I won't stir a step unless you come, too," Sally Day told her.

"Sarah, go along. I want to get this done."

"No. You need fresh air. If you don't come then you'll keep me home, and that would be right mean!"

Mrs. Horne said reluctantly, "I guess it's easier to give in than to argue with the likes of you, though I did aim to finish the carding before night."

Once they were on the road though, her step quickened and she threw back her head to catch the sun, clasping her shawl around her, for there was still a nip in the air. They walked east and came to the broad meadow that belonged to Sally Day and Charles. Sally Day wanted to cross the field to see if it was greening a little bit along the brook but Mrs. Horne warned her she mustn't get her feet wet and catch cold.

"That's where we thought of building," Sally Day said, pointing out a tall beech sheltering a group of slim birches.

"Are you terribly disappointed you probably won't be building this spring, Sarah? Or hasn't Charles had the heart to tell you?"

"He didn't tell me, but I guessed, and yes, I'm terribly disappointed."

"Well, all of us have to get used to disappointments, for they're what we get most of in this life."

Sally Day faced her. "Do you honestly believe that, Mother? Do you think it's all laid out beforehand, and we can't change it? Don't you want to believe that we have some say about what happens to us?"

"Why I'd never thought about that."

Sally Day forgot how she'd promised herself she'd obey in all things and be mealymouthed and mild in her speech. She said vigorously, "If I couldn't believe I had some say about what happens to me then I'd want to die!"

"God ordains the time of our death."

It was so intoxicating to be really talking and sharing thoughts, Sally Day threw caution to the winds. "Let God decide when we're to die," she said recklessly, "just so long as while we're still alive we manage our own fate and don't let life whiffle us around willy-nilly."

Mrs. Horne chuckled. "Small chance of you being whiffled around, Sarah. I never knew such a body for asserting herself. I declare, home's a livelier place since you came, I'll say that for it!"

Sally Day threw her arms around Elizabeth and hugged her. "Oh, I do believe I'm beginning to love you!" she cried.

"I wish you could begin to love Mr. Horne."

They were being so frank, Sally Day went too far. "That's up to him, I guess, whether he wants folks to love him. He seems to think the farm is some kind of a jail. That's what it's been to me all winter, anyway. I get so scared Charles will take after him I'd like to die sometimes. Charles and I are so different as night and day anyway and if he turns out like Mr. Horne then I'll be caught in a trap forever—"

She stopped. The look on the older woman's face cut her short. Mrs. Horne looked absolutely stricken and she whispered, "Sarah, Sarah, don't say such things. You cut the ground right out from under my feet when you talk so."

Sally Day took her arm, looking up into her face anxiously, afraid she had hurt her very badly. They turned homeward. Mrs. Horne was trembling, and Sally Day saw what an effort of will it took her to keep control of herself.

They had almost reached the house when Mrs. Horne stopped in the road. "You married a good man, Sarah," she said in a low voice. "Charles is a good man."

"Oh, I know that, I never said he wasn't!"

"You married him, so you've made your own bed and you'll just have to learn to lie in it."

Not another word would Mrs. Horne say. She withdrew where Sally Day could not reach her. That day and the next they worked together side by side, doing the homely tasks that were so familiar. Mrs. Horne answered only in monosyllables, and sorrowfully Sally Day realized that her mother-in-law had spoken the truth, that Sally Day had cut the ground from under Elizabeth Horne's feet by criticizing Ezra.

One thing Mrs. Horne had said was not true, though, no it was not, Sally Day told herself. Yes, she had made her own bed. No, she did not have to lie in it, not at least until she had made every effort to improve it!

She pictured to herself in such detail the new life she and Charles would have when they moved to Maryland, it became real. They would build a little house, perhaps near the canal. Anytime she felt like it she would go home for an hour to visit with her mother. She would have the pleasure of watching Willie and Gene growing up. When the baby came she would take him often so they could all have the joy of sharing him.

In their own little house where she and Charles lived there would be sunshine and warmth and laughter. They would leave the cold and the silence behind them forever.

The letter finally came, but it was from her mother. "Papa will write you soon, but I couldn't wait another day," Mrs. Hammond wrote. "Oh, what happiness your letter gave us, my darling! Yes, there is a place in the store for Charles, and your father truly needs him. It's a good business, and it worries him that years will pass before Eugene is old enough to take over.

"Sally Day, dear, why should you build a home some-where else when there's the cottage right next door beyond the orchard? It's stood empty for years. I'm surprised you forgot about it, for it could easily be fixed up and made comfortable and cozy, and is just the right size for you and Charles and the baby that's on the way.

"We are so glad you and Charles want to come, though we are sorry you have been so unhappy up North. My heart aches to think how his parents will grieve to lose you both, but you and your husband would not enter into this plan without knowing it is right, and we can only rejoice we will have you near us."

Sally Day laughed and cried with relief. Now only one thing remained to be done. Charles had to be told.

Chapter Eighteen

S HE DECIDED TO be patient, to wait for exactly the right time, the right opportunity. It didn't come that day or the next, for all day long Charles was away from the house, cutting trees in the wood lot and finishing the mending of the walls. When he came in at night, the four Hornes were together in the kitchen. After she and Charles went up to bed came Sally Day's only chance to talk, but Charles was so tired he fell asleep before she finished brushing and braiding her hair.

No, this plan couldn't be put before Charles in a few moments Sally Day happened to find. Thursday night when the two went to choir practice gave them their only real time together.

Charles didn't care whether they went or not, and when the next Thursday evening came he fussed that the March wind was chilly and Sally Day might catch cold, that the buggy's springs needed replacing and the jolting would be bad for her. "Charles, that's nonsense," she told him. "I've just got to get out, and I'm strong as a horse anyway, and I'll never have a healthy, strong baby if you insist on wrapping me in cotton wool."

He said no more, and seemed relieved that the docile,

quiet little wife had vanished and his lively one with the sparkling eyes was back again.

They discovered when they set out that a full moon had laid a silver sheen over the brown countryside. Sally Day said, "Let's not hurry. It won't matter if we're a little late."

She shivered with nervousness under the buffalo robe. Now that the moment had come she was scared to death. She went on, "Besides, I want to talk to you."

"Talk away," he said, slowing Ebenezer with a pull on the reins.

For days she had planned exactly how she was going to tell him, but now that the time had come her orderly arguments went right out of her head. She blurted out her true feelings, and began by telling him how she despaired of their ever finding happiness living in his parents' home. "Why, I almost died of misery this past awful winter," she said.

She felt him stiffen and pressed closer against him. "There's a way out, Charles," she went on hurriedly. "I reckon I'd better tell you first that I'm sorry I may have deceived you a little bit, but I had to make sure. My father is ready to welcome you into his business. He wants to make you a partner. My folks would like to give us the cottage next to their own home."

She clasped his arm. "Charles, I know you would love that kind of a life. Really, dearest, nobody who has a choice would take this hard life we've got up here! Isn't it a wonderful thing that we do have a choice?"

They had reached the edge of town. "Now maybe we'd better hurry Ebenezer so we won't be too late for choir," she said. "I don't ask you to make your mind up right this minute, dearest. Take your time and then when you're ready we'll talk about it again."

Charles said nothing. They arrived in front of the church. Buggies were tied in the shed and the church lights glowed. Charles kept going.

"Why didn't you turn in?" Sally Day asked.

He drove straight through town and out the other end. Finally he pulled off the road and turned to her. "I don't see how we could be married all these months and know each other so little," he said despairingly.

"That's not so!" Sally Day exclaimed. "We're very close and I love you to pieces!"

"The minister's words were supposed to make us one."

"And they did."

"No, Sally Day, they did not. You have worked behind my back to get your own way. You let me believe you were really trying to be a helpmate. Now I wonder if you were only play-acting, deceiving me right from the beginning, planning something like this."

"Charles, I give you my word, it only occurred to me about three weeks ago." Sally Day began to cry. "I did try! I tried hard all winter long and what good did it do me?"

Charles pushed her over on her own side of the buggy seat and sat for a long time staring out over the moonlit fields. His face looked as though it was carved out of granite, and Sally Day shivered. In the profile of his young face she saw the beginnings of the pointed chin, the sharp nose that gave his father's a hawklike look.

She watched him, scarcely breathing, waiting for him to speak. Finally he said, "My father is right, there can be only one master in a house. If a man lets his woman rule, then he is nothing. We'll go on as we were.

"I'll build you a house when I'm able to afford it, Sally

Day. I won't borrow, for a farmer who takes on the burden of a debt is a slave forever after.

"I can't manage it this spring, but when summer comes and the work slacks off in mid-season, then I'll take you to Maryland for a week's visit with your people."

There didn't seem to be much love in his voice as he said harshly, "You're not the first woman who married and then decided she'd made a mistake, and you won't be the last. Perhaps you should have married your cousin, who would amuse you and dance attendance on you. Instead you married me, and this is my home, so it's your home, too, and our child's. So here you stay, and you'd do well to begin to make the best of it." He clucked to Ebenezer and turned the buggy in the narrow road.

Sally Day was so frightened her heart lurched in her breast. She had never meant to stir up any such storm as this. She hadn't dreamed she would hurt Charles so badly that in the space of one evening his love would turn to hate.

They drove past the church. Jane Cope and Frederick Allenton, Jane's new beau, were just arriving. They were laughing together as Frederick put up his arms to help her down. Jane saw the Hornes and called, "Hello, you two, you're late, have you been courting in the moonlight?" Charles drove on without giving them so much as a glance.

Sometimes, in the miserable days that followed, Sally Day thought hysterically, I wish I would die. If I died, then Charles would be good and sorry! She went alone to the woods with only Duke for company, and wept for hours at a time.

Mrs. Horne must have guessed that something very serious had gone wrong between the young people, but she didn't ask questions and for that Sally Day was grateful.

She was grateful, too, that she could depend on Charles's loyalty not to talk to his parents. Give the devil his due, she thought, he's loyal. He knows it would just about kill me if he told. Besides he's got his pride and doesn't want to lose face either.

It would have been more fitting if winter had come back with its bitter winds and cold and misery. Instead, as the days lengthened, a balmy feeling came over the land. The air smelled earthy and fresh and new, the rain fell gently.

Sally Day often caught Mrs. Horne watching her anxiously, and once she said, "Surely the skunk cabbage is up now, Sarah, and the pussy willows are out. Why don't we walk to the swamp and see?"

"No, thank you," Sally Day said dully.

"Are you feeling poorly, child?"

"I don't feel well and that's a fact, but I'll get over it."

"Suppose we go to town and see Dr. Strong. He might have something better than my sulphur and molasses to perk you up."

Sally Day considered Mrs. Horne and Dr. Strong two very clever people and she had no intention of letting them pry into her feelings, for she was afraid they might worm the truth out of her. She mustered a smile and said, "I don't need a tonic, Mother. I reckon all I need is a dose of spring flowers and seeing the birds come back."

"Well, now, I expect if we go for a little walk we just might see the first robin."

"I don't really feel like walking."

Sally Day didn't mope all the time. Sometimes she had bursts of energy. One of these struck her on a brisk, windy morning, and she stripped their bed, opened the window wide and propped it up with a stick and hung all the bedding out to air. She was struggling with the feather mattress, trying to turn it, when she heard a buggy's tires singing in the road.

She idly went to the window to look. Sure enough the buggy turned in, swaying from side to side up the rocky lane. A young man she had never seen before jumped down. Mr. Horne had gone to town to see about buying a new plow, and Charles was clearing stones from the fields with the stone boat. Mrs. Horne emerged from the house to see what the stranger wanted.

"Is the man of the house at home?" he asked.

Sally Day heard her mother-in-law's answer. "No, my husband's in town, but my son's on the place somewhere. Suppose you state your business."

Sally Day had to smile for the young man sounded like a real smooth talker. "Ma'am, I represent a new line of miraculous patent medicines that will cure anything and everything overnight that ails your animals. Would you like your hens to increase their laying? I've got a powder that'll double their eggs and make them lay bigger ones. Do your horses ever go lame? My liniment will put them on their feet and raring to go. Any of your cows ever swell up with the bloat? Ma'am, my magical pill—"

"You stop that this minute," Mrs. Horne's voice cut in. "You get yourself and your buggy out of here. We don't need your worthless stuff."

"Do you mind if I just sit here and wait for your menfolks to show up?"

"Yes, I do mind. We've been cheated by your kind before, and I want you off this place."

"Then I'll just wait out in the road, because that's a public highway and so it's free."

"Wait where you want to but it won't do you any good. Just get off this place." Mrs. Horne picked up the pail of slops and disappeared into the barn.

What Sally Day did then had no thought behind it whatsoever. She acted on pure instinct. She watched the salesman turn his rig, heard it clatter down the lane, saw him pull up to water his horse a hundred yards from the gate where the brook crossed the road. She slipped out of her calico dress and into a trousseau dress she could still wear and threw her cloak around her. She darted out the side door and ran down the lane. She had snatched up her reticule before she left her room. She felt inside a side pocket. Yes, there was the leather purse containing some of the money her father had given her for a wedding present.

The salesman saw her coming and leaped from the buggy to meet her. "Oh, please, will you take me to town? I'll pay you!" Sally Day gasped.

"Are you running away?"

"Yes."

He grinned, his eyes widening with admiration. "From that old battleaxe? Are you her hired girl? You don't look like any hired girl! Say, if her husband's as sour as she is, I don't blame you. Up you go!" He boosted Sally Day up to the high seat.

He picked up the reins and started off, but kept glancing down at her. "You're too pretty a little thing to work in somebody else's house, you ought to have a husband and home of your own," he said.

"Oh, please, won't you hurry?"

"Why? You afraid the old man'll follow and make you go back? All right." He slapped the reins on the horse's back and it quickened its steps.

They rounded a curve and then the Horne farm was out of sight. Sally Day remembered that her father-in-law had gone to Jericho on business. What if they met him on the road?

"Where are you going when you get to town?" the stranger asked.

"To the depot. The train comes through at noon."

"And then where?"

"I'm going home to Maryland."

He whistled. "You're a long ways from home. How come you're working way up here?"

Sally Day clutched the bar in front of her because the swaying combined with her fright made her sick. "It's a long story and I haven't time to tell it. If we get there in time to catch the train I'll pay you a dollar."

With that he flicked the horse between the ears with his thin whip. It broke into a gallop. "I won't take your dollar. It'll be enough of a reward to help a beautiful lady in distress!" he shouted gallantly.

He slowed down when he reached Main Street. The depot was at the other end. Sally Day had pulled her hood down to cover her face, so that no one would recognize her. They reached Strong's General Store. She peeped out from under her hood and saw that Ezra Horne was standing on the porch of the store. He stared at the salesman's buggy as anyone would, noticing a strange rig. Sally Day saw him stiffen. She didn't look back, but she thought he had recognized her.

The young man drew up with a flourish at the depot, the buggy sending out a cloud of dust. He jumped out and took her in his arms and set her on her feet. She had a silver dollar clasped in her sweating hand, and tried to put it in his but he refused it. "I'll wait and see you safely aboard," he offered.

"Oh, no, please don't. Thank you very much," Sally Day said earnestly. "I'll never forget the big favor you've done me."

"All right, if that's the way you want it." She hurried to the door and heard him go off whistling, pleased he'd done a good deed.

Eph Stone had watched her arrival and gawked through the bars of his ticket window. Sally Day put her hand over her heart, trying to still its wild beating. "Good morning, Eph," she said. "Would you sell me a ticket, please, to New York?"

"Yes, sure I will. You going to New York alone?"

"I'm going home to visit my folks in Maryland. Would you tell me how much it will cost if I take the cars to Elkton, Maryland? From there I'll go by stage."

It seemed to Sally Day he took hours to study the book that told about trains, but finally he added up the amounts and she breathed a sigh of relief, for her reticule held enough money. She managed a wavery smile.

He gave her the ticket. "Who was that young feller that drove you in?" he asked. "How come your husband didn't fetch you to town?"

"The young man happened to be at the farm and Charles was busy," she explained.

Eph didn't look as though this explanation sounded reasonable to him.

"I just about made it, didn't I?" she said, and this time she gave the station master the benefit of her very best smile.

He blinked, somewhat dazzled, then said, "Oh, no, you've plenty of time. The train's due in fifteen minutes, but the telegraph just let me know it's forty minutes late. It's been held up somewheres along the line."

"Oh, dear," Sally Day whispered.

"Mis' Horne, where's your satchel?"

"My satchel? Oh, I didn't bring one. I'm only going for a short visit. I guess I'll sit outside and wait. It's so warm in here."

She found a place on an upturned box and sat down. She smoothed her hair with the comb from her reticule and tidied her dress and buttoned her cloak. She was trying not to think. She kept her eyes on the shining rails running north from Jericho, praying to see a puff of smoke in the distance.

Maybe that hour wasn't a lifetime, but only seemed like one. At last, far off, she heard a musical note, saw a thin puff of smoke rising above the low hills. Eph opened the station door and called, "Train's coming, Mis' Horne. You're the only passenger, so I'll put up the flag to tell it to stop."

The train crept closer, tooting for each crossing. It shot sparks and smoke from its wide funnel as it slowed for the depot. Eph was at Sally Day's elbow to help her up the steps. "Have a nice visit and come back soon," he told her.

She found a seat in the first car she entered, still keeping her hood pulled over her head. She heard Mr. Stone call to the engineer, "All ready, let her roll!" Then he shouted, "No, stop!" He was too late for the train had started to move.

Sally Day peeped out from under her hood. A buggy was coming at full gallop down Main Street, its driver standing and whipping the horse. He reached the depot and flung himself out.

Sally Day twisted around, peering through the dirty window. Charles was desperately running after the train, his face scarlet, contorted by the effort. He caught the hand-rail by the steps. For a few seconds it was touch and go whether he could hang on.

Sally Day stood up and started for the door to help him, to save him. Before she reached him, Charles had found safe footing on the steps and swung himself aboard.

Chapter Nineteen

S HE HELPED HIM along the aisle and he sank down on the wooden seat gasping, trying to get air into his lungs. He drew in a long breath and said, "Where in blazes do you think you're going?"

"I'm going home to Maryland."

He glared at her with no love in his eyes. "You landed us in a mess and made a spectacle of us before the whole town. Here I am in my work clothes aboard a train going I don't know where and not a cent in my pocket."

The conductor was interested in that fact. He had been standing beside their seat, listening. "How far you going?" he asked.

"To the next stop," Charles told him.

"That would be Norwich."

Sally Day handed him her own ticket. "This says New York," he noted.

"It says New York but it doesn't mean New York," Charles rasped. "She's getting off at the next stop, too, so there'll be money due us on her ticket."

"Well, now, I don't know about that," the conductor drawled. "It seems she bought her ticket, so it's up to her where she gets off."

177

"She gets off at Norwich! I'm her husband so take my word for it!" Charles shouted for everybody in the car to hear.

With no more argument the conductor gave Charles what was due if Sally Day got off in Norwich, received the price of Charles's ticket, and walked on grinning and shaking his head.

Charles acted as though he was out of his mind. He grasped Sally Day's wrist so hard she cried out from the pain. "Now will you please explain this craziness to me?"

"I was going home. I couldn't stand it in that awful house one more day."

"Did anybody beat you there?" Charles demanded.

"No."

"Were you fed?"

"Yes."

"Were you warm?"

"Yes."

"You admit all that. Then what excuse did you have for running off?"

Sally Day let out a cry of grief. "I can't stay in a house where nobody loves me!"

She sensed from the stillness in the car that the other passengers were drinking in every word, but like Charles she didn't care.

"Who says nobody loves you?" Charles demanded.

"I do."

"I love you and you know it!"

"I don't know any such thing. You act as though you hate me."

Charles tried to brush his hair down with his hand. He picked at his clothes and growled, "I stink of the barn. This is a fine thing! I never would have believed you'd land me in a mess like this." Sally Day handed him the comb from her reticule. He combed his hair, then he returned to the quarrel. "You knew I'd follow you."

"I didn't know any such thing. I didn't want you to." Sally Day lifted her chin defiantly.

"You knew I'd follow. You thought you'd get your own way. You figured I'd give up the land that's mine, that I'd take a job working in a store, inside all day, never getting any fresh air, a lackey in somebody else's business. What kind of a life is that for a man who owns two hundred acres of good sweet land?" Charles was working up a real rage again, and Sally Day put her hand on his to quiet him. He seized her fingers and wrung them.

He was an absolute stranger. She felt she had never laid eyes before on this man. Words tumbled out, from her silent Charles. "You don't know anything about men. You haven't got a brain in your head!" he shouted. "Are all women as stupid as you are?"

Somebody at the end of the car called, "They're all cut out of the same cloth," and another sang out, "Hear, hear! Give it to her, young feller."

"Now see what you've gone and done," Sally Day wailed. "You've made fools of both of us."

This new Charles didn't seem to care one bit. He drew a long breath, then stated, "You married me legally. Even without a brain in your head I love you. You weren't just running off alone, you were taking my child with you. You and I married each other for a lifetime and that's a lot of years." He stopped.

For the first time in her life Sally Day was stricken dumb. The two sat side by side, her hand clasped in his. Sally Day was looking down that vista of years. She was so ashamed she wanted to curl up and die. The minister had said, "For better or for worse," and those words were holy, like all the others that made her and Charles one.

The train went clickety-clack running through a patch of woods. Dry eyed, Sally Day stared out of the window. The tracks were paralleling a brook and she saw that along its edges green was showing. The pale sun slanted through bare trees that would soon be heavy and green with leaves.

She had been fleeing toward home, toward the spring of the year and away from the harsh land that was Connecticut in winter. She thought, confused, if I'd stayed, spring would have caught up with me.

"Charles, I don't know what to say," she whispered.

"You could start with 'I'm sorry,'" he told her.

"I'm sorry."

They clasped hands and rode in silence for awhile. Charles broke it. "I'm sorry, too," he said in a low voice. "I didn't try hard enough to put myself in your shoes. I see better now, how hard it was. Sally Day, we'll break ground this spring for our own house. I guess my trouble was, I took a foolish pride in not asking Pa for a loan. He'll give us the money, I know that. My land, he was about out of his mind when he rushed home to tell me you'd gone! We may start small, with only three rooms, and add on later as our family grows. But our child will be born in his own house."

"Thank you, Charles," Sally Day whispered. For just a minute she remembered she must write her parents they would not be moving to Maryland after all.

The train wheezed into the Norwich depot and they got off. All the passengers stared openly, and one middle-aged woman reached out and touched Sally Day's arm. "You're doing the right thing, dear," she said. "He's a good man. Don't run away from him again."

They found they would have to wait half the day for a train to take them home. Sally Day was ready to faint with hunger. She gave Charles all the money in her bag, and he escorted her to Norwich's elegant hotel for dinner. It didn't bother him that his muddy boots marred the fine carpet and he smelled of the barn. He ate a big dinner and ordered her to eat, too, although when the food came she was afraid all the excitement would make her sick.

They got on the train at five and rode home. Eph's eyes bugged out when he saw them descending the train steps. "You didn't make a very long visit to Maryland, Mis' Horne," he remarked.

Sally smiled slightly but she didn't answer.

When they started off in the buggy, Charles put his arm around Sally Day to hold her steady on the seat, but he didn't kiss her or show he was holding her because he loved her.

"Oh, dear, I haven't got the courage to face your father," Sally Day cried, trying to hold her husband back when they drove into the yard.

"Yes, you have. A girl who's got the nerve to run off and abandon her husband to fend for herself and her unborn child has got the courage to face anything," Charles said.

Lamplight was streaming through the kitchen window, and Sally Day could see her husband's face. He was smiling, and he wore a look that she recognized as triumphant.

He opened the door for her. Mrs. Horne got up from the table and rushed to take Sally Day in her arms. She led Sally Day to a chair and put her into it. "I'll fetch you a cup of tea. You must be fainting with hunger."

Charles was washing at the sink. He looked as though he felt about seven feet tall and he still wore that triumphant smile.

Mr. Horne pushed his plate away and leaned back in his chair, surveying his daughter-in-law. "I don't know what the fuss is all about," he said. "You came back."

Sally Day was too tired to do more than nod.

"I suppose you feel like a heroine in one of those romantical novels you sometimes sneak into the house," he observed.

She shook her head.

"You made a fool out of my son."

Charles startled them all then by challenging his father. "No, Pa, she didn't make any fool out of me," he said. "A man can only do that to himself. She got mixed up in her mind and ran off, but now she's back. It won't happen again."

"How do you know it won't happen again?"

"She belongs here. She knows it now. That right, Sally Day?"

Sally Day nodded. The idea did occur to her that when she got rested up some, and got over the fright and excitement of this long day, she wouldn't sit like a ninny listening to her husband and his father sitting in judgment on her. But that could wait for another day. Now she only wanted to drink her tea and climb the stairs to her own bed and sleep and sleep.

Charles was almost swaggering, and he repeated, "That right, Sally Day? You won't ever run away again?"

She started to nod, then stopped. "I don't make any promises. I'll see how things go."

Charles had been acting much too sure of himself and he

gawked at her. It was the father who answered for the son. "I don't reckon you'll run off and make a success of it," he told Sally Day, "because I won't allow it neither." He scowled so hard his bushy brows met. "I've been doing some thinking today," he growled. "It was quiet enough around here with you gone so a man could do some thinking. Did it ever occur to you, young miss, the rest of us don't mind having you around?

"Oh, yes, you're noisy and you're disrupting. That's what you are, you're a disrupting influence around here. But you married my son, and so you joined up with the Hornes. You're not a Hammond any more, you're a Horne now. Sarah Horne."

He snorted then. "If you set real store by it, maybe some day I'll manage to get my tongue around that name of yours, Sally Day. Sounds like the name of some milksop heroine in one of those novels!"

Sally Day began uncertainly, "Well, I reckon if you can put up with me then I can put up with you folks, Mr. Horne."

He wasn't finished. He said, "My son acts so easy going, he fooled you. Charles was at Antietam, and a man who fought at Antietam isn't likely to be afraid of any half-pint gal."

"No, I guess not, Mr. Horne." Sally Day swayed in her chair, too tired to hold her head up any longer. Mrs. Horne took charge then, and lifted her and half carried her up the stairs. The last Sally Day heard from the men was Charles's voice, "Pa, I'm starting on the cellar hole for my house tomorrow. I'll need your help."

Mrs. Horne didn't say a word until Sally Day was safely in bed. Then she put her arms around her and whispered, "Sarah, I'm so thankful. I just couldn't face it, thinking I was going to be alone again, the only woman in this family."

She took the candle away, leaving Sally Day.

Charles would be up soon, and maybe he would want to talk some more, and there wasn't anything left to say. Maybe tomorrow when she was rested, Sally Day would think of some things to say, but not tonight. She would pretend she was asleep.

Mrs. Horne had opened the window. Sally Day lay quiet, listening for her husband's step, longing to hear it, so thankful he had brought her back home she felt like weeping again but she was plumb out of tears. She was listening so hard she heard a new sound coming through the window.

Peepers! Off there in the swamp, the peepers had started, sending their shrill little cries into the calm April night, announcing that spring had finally and officially arrived.

Sally Day was already half asleep but she had one more thought, and it was a poetical one: I ran away from winter, and ran home to spring.

About the Author

Born in New Milford, Connecticut in 1908, Bianca Bradbury lived in the state of Connecticut throughout her life. As a young wife, her writing took the form of verse, articles and short stories, which found their way into such magazines as *Family Circle* and *McCall's*. After the birth of her two sons, she began writing for children, first picture books, and then longer books. Later, when the boys had grown up and left home, Mrs. Bradbury's fiction focused mostly on contemporary issues for young adults. Besides a love for animals, which is most evident in her books for younger readers, her novels reveal her deep interest in honestly dealing with the realities of life. She was never afraid of tackling controversial subjects, desiring to do so with integrity and hope.

Flight into Spring, while aimed at older readers as many of Bianca Bradbury's later books were, is different from these because of its historical setting. It beautifully succeeds in showing the author's view that to persevere through the day-to-day difficulties of life and relationship is both necessary and possible and was as true in times past as it is today.

Bianca Bradbury's sons recall the life-long discipline she exhibited in her writing craft and her happy zest for life—both important attributes in writers for the young. She authored 46 books over a span of 40 years. Mrs. Bradbury died in 1982.

Young Adult Historical Bookshelf

The Young Adult Historical Bookshelf is designed to provide intelligent reading for thoughtful teenagers. These titles deal with the more complex issues that young people encounter in the process of growing up. They are presented in a historical context and the world view is less harsh than the modern "teen" or "adult" novel. Bethlehem Books believes that books for this age level can continue to be uplifting, while touching on the realms of romance, death, and coming of age.

TITLES IN THIS SERIES

Beyond the Desert Gate, by Mary Ray
The Borrowed House, by Hilda van Stockum
Brave Buffalo Fighter, by John D. Fitzgerald
Downright Dencey, by Caroline Dale Snedeker
Flight into Spring, by Bianca Bradbury
The Ides of April, by Mary Ray
My Heart Lies South, by Elizabeth Borton de Trevino
The Rose Round, by Meriol Trevor
Under a Changing Moon, by Margot Benary-Isbert
With Pipe, Paddle and Song, by Elizabeth Yates
They Loved to Laugh, by Kathryn Worth